A Geordie by birth, John   moved to
East Anglia with his fam   at the age of
twelve. He   lives in the region, the setting
for mos   books. "It's wide and bleak,"
he s   what looks plain is really full of
mys   en I look out   ss the vast
expa   Fens it's like   at a great
blank   to be wri   " After
servin   luring t!   World
War,   ourr   fic-
tior n   widely rec-
ognized   in   ntemporary
write   ural. His
book: *Hill, The
Giant*   the   *use on the
Brin*   *Burnin*   *ther Ghosts,
Gi* *Ghost, The* *er Watch* and
the   eenage Memo   *nary Seaman*.
Married with two gro   up children, he lives
near Norwich.

Books by the same author

The Burning Baby and Other Ghosts

Catch Your Death, and Other Stories

The Ghost on the Hill

Gilray's Ghost

The Grasshopper

The House on the Brink

Ordinary Seaman (autobiography)

The Spitfire Grave and Other Stories

The Waterfall Box

THE
FLESH
EATER

JOHN GORDON

WALKER BOOKS
AND SUBSIDIARIES
LONDON · BOSTON · SYDNEY

For Dennis
After all, he's no vegetarian.

First published 1998 by Walker Books Ltd
87 Vauxhall Walk, London SE11 5HJ

This edition published 1998

2 4 6 8 10 9 7 5 3 1

Text © 1998 John Gordon
Cover Illustration © 1998 Julek Heller

The right of John Gordon to be identified as author of this
book has been asserted by him in accordance with the
Copyright, Design and Patents Act 1988.

This book has been typeset in Sabon.

Printed in England

British Library Cataloguing in Publication Data
A catalogue record for this book is available
from the British Library.

ISBN 0-7445-6073-X

CHAPTER ONE

The air in the Crescent was warm and still and so charged with summer that girls stirred golden dust whenever they moved. Especially one.

"My mother says I've got duck's disease," said Miranda Merchant. "My bottom's too big and I waddle when I walk."

"I've never noticed."

"But it's true, Harry. Look." She took a pace ahead of him, pulling her short jacket tight around her waist to emphasize her rear, and she walked with her toes turned in. "See what I mean?"

He saw what she meant.

"And big feet," she said.

"Terrible feet," he agreed. "I wondered how you got those tiny shoes on." The shoes fitted snugly over her toes and small heels.

"It's congenital," said Miranda. "My mother is just the same."

"It's just something you'll have to live with."

Mrs Merchant was startlingly good-looking and Harry, living where he did, often saw her.

"So you see, Harry, I do have my bad points."

He had been telling her the opposite, but he made no reply. He was thinking that only the really beautiful, such as Miranda and her mother, could afford to admit defects. Like the very rich, they could play at being poor.

"Harry?" Miranda stopped and stood in front of him. "I want to know what's in your mind."

"You both are – you and your mother."

She raised her eyebrows.

"You are both similar in one respect." He was taking a risk.

"Surely you're not going to tell a girl she's the same as her mother!"

"I'm afraid so. You are both callipygian."

"Callipy-what?"

"It means having a beautiful behind, like Aphrodite."

"And to think I have to sit on it," she said.

They were in the Crescent, taking the long way round to wherever it was they would eventually decide to go. On one side the Crescent was a long curve of tall houses, but on the other there was a high wall that hid the gardens of Barbican House. Very little traffic came this way and Harry was leaning forward to kiss Miranda, and she was not unwilling, when her eyes detected something behind him.

A car drifted by, but it was not that which had

disturbed her. At the centre of the curve of house-fronts a girl had emerged.

Her appearance amused Harry. "She looks flustered," he said. "Is someone after her?"

"And why not?" Miranda defended the girl. "Emma Judd is very nice-looking."

That was beauty being generous again. "She's a wreck," said Harry. The girl wore a cardigan that was half-off one shoulder and she was tugging at it as she came towards them clutching a pile of books.

"Look who's talking," said Miranda. "When have you been so smart, Harry Hogge?"

Emma Judd's hair was tied at the back, but unintended wisps clung to her forehead and cheeks. "Did you hear anything?" she gasped. "Did you hear it?" And then she had to concentrate to prevent the books spilling from her arms.

Miranda waited until the books were safe before she asked, "Hear what?"

"Listen!" Emma struggled to get her breath. "There! Did you hear!"

Miranda shook her head, but the girl's eyes were on Harry, beseeching him to agree. "No," he said bluntly. "It's all quiet."

His rebuff startled her, and for a moment she was so round-eyed and innocently childish, so dependent on him, that he turned his head away. She had no right to make him feel brutal, and his attitude showed it.

Miranda put him to shame. She was beginning

to ask Emma what had frightened her when there was a clatter of falling books and Harry looked round to see the girl with her hands over her ears and whispering, "It was awful! They were saying terrible things!"

Miranda had an arm around Emma's shoulders, and Harry stooped to pick up the books. He had to show some sympathy so he said, "There's a bit of a buzz in the air ... I can hear that."

Emma lifted her head and listened. "Yes," she said. "There is a buzz."

"It's traffic." He pointed beyond the walled garden towards the houses in the centre of the town. "The market place is busy."

She nodded, wanting to agree. "That's all there is now, just a hum ... but a minute ago I heard people talking."

He looked up at the curve of housefronts. "It's like a dish," he told her. "A big ear that magnifies things."

"Exactly!" Miranda was being helpful. "I can imagine it, too."

"I suppose so." Emma took a deep breath and her glance flickered across their faces but could not remain steady. "I'm making a fool of myself. The trouble is, I was with my aunt and she heard it, too." Now she looked up, determined to put it aside. "Two hysterical women, isn't that it? Encouraging each other, making things worse."

"Your aunt?" said Miranda. "Where is she?"

Emma pointed back to where the curve of the

Crescent was pierced by an archway that led to a tangle of alleyways in the old part of the town. "She lives there, and we were outside her house when suddenly she said she heard these voices – and then I heard them. Two people, a man and a woman, and they were plotting something." She paused, embarrassed, and then went on calmly, as if she was telling them about a film. "They said they had to put someone out of the way, and the man said he'd do it." Her eyes widened, and suddenly she was again believing what she had heard. "There's going to be a murder … tonight!"

Her certainty revived Harry's scorn. "You heard someone's radio," he said. "People don't plot murders in broad daylight in loud voices."

"There was no radio. And the voices did not come from anywhere." With her free hand Emma gathered her hair away from her face and held it bunched on top of her head. It was a pose that, for a moment, made her elegant, and her face was haughty and beautiful. "I heard voices," she said. "Mad people hear voices. I heard two people say they were going to get rid of someone, and I believed it. That makes me mad." She turned her eyes first on Miranda and then on Harry as if challenging them to disprove it.

"Everyone gets a bit confused at times," said Miranda.

Emma Judd smiled. "But not like me. I heard what I heard, and I heard it distinctly. I even heard the name of the man they are after. Dorman.

A man called Dorman."

Her voice was as cool as the marble of her cheeks. She turned and left them.

Watching her go, Miranda said, "Well, I hope I'm not around when she freaks out like that again."

"Do you think she will?"

"How would I know?"

"You might."

"I know one thing, Harry Hogge. It worked quite well for her – that pale little face and those big grey eyes of hers. They got you interested."

"With you around … how could I be?"

"Because I'm…" Provoking him, she tightened her jacket over her hips.

"Beautiful-bottomed," he said. He paused and then added, "And I'm not the only one to think so."

"Oh, not that again." She raised her eyes to the sky. "How many more times do I have to tell you that it's all over between him and me? I don't like him."

"But you did."

"Harry Hogge." He noticed she had her hands clasped together tightly but he could not know she was struggling to prevent herself tugging his jacket straight, doing up a button, brushing his shoulders. "You might be big, but you are very stupid. You exasperate me. Be quiet and listen… You live in the biggest hotel in town but, to look at you, nobody would believe it, and you never take advantage of it. I don't believe you've ever taken a girl there and given her coffee."

"Only because…" He broke off. "Oh hell, Miranda, that would be a cheap thing to do, wouldn't it?"

"Anyone else would love to impress a girl." There was a gleam in her eye as she smiled at him. "Do you know the only person who's ever taken me there?"

"I can guess."

"Well then," she said, "and Donovan Brett is a pig."

"You didn't always think so. And he's a reasonable kind of guy." And, he had to admit to himself, Donovan Brett was handsome; very.

"But you are not a girl. I detest him." She forced him to look at her. "I really dislike him. Now are you satisfied?"

"Miranda," he said, "would you like to have coffee with me in the Pheasant and Trumpet?"

"I thought you'd never ask."

"That's because I'm mad."

"Mad as Emma Judd?"

"Well," he said, "not quite as mad as that … and I wonder which Mr Dorman it is who's going to be done to death."

"That," said Miranda happily, "is something we shall never know."

CHAPTER TWO

The only light in the room came from the shaded lamp over the card table where a woman was playing solitaire. She was alone in Barbican House and the only sound was the soft tap and flutter of the cards as she dealt and played.

She shuffled the deck once more. She was dexterous but unhurried. Her fingers were smooth and pale, and the polished nails gleamed brighter than the single heavy ring that glinted from time to time under the lamp, but it was impossible to tell her age from her hands. Her face was in shadow.

She dealt and paused to study the faces of the cards. She was as intense as a general bowed over a map in his tent, and when she spoke her voice was so soft it died in the shadows of the room.

"The cards are secretive tonight," she said.

Beyond the town, where the jagged peaks of rooftops and spires against the night sky had given place to the open countryside, a solitary cyclist made his way along a straight road where no other traffic ran and the only sound was the faint sigh of his wheels. He carried no lights, but the stars showed him the verges and the deeper darkness of the dykes which bordered the road on either side.

"There is no one to see where I go," he said.

In the house the woman looked up as if some sound had distracted her, but the room was silent. "And I am alone in this great house behind the wall until you return," she murmured.

"Poor prisoner." His voice was caressing.

"Your willing prisoner," she said. "I have leave to go where I will, but I choose to stay. We need nothing but each other, my love."

"We two against the world," he said.

"Two together ... as always." She bent once more to her cards. "Their faces tease me tonight, my dear, but they are not unkind."

The cyclist, muttering into the air as he rode, said, "And this machine is a revelation. Cycling could become a passion with me. All is well."

"Take care, the cards are uncertain."

The cyclist was in good humour. "I am a horse thief. I cut the padlock and stuffed the bolt cutters into a hedge, mounted my silent stolen steed and rode away. Fear not, my love, no one saw me leave, and there is no car to trace."

She turned the cards, listening beyond the shadows in the room. "You are almost there," she said.

In the flat landscape, squat orchard trees crowded close to the road, standing in darkness like black cattle penned by the dykes, but ahead of him a pinprick of light gleamed as if to emphasize the loneliness of the place. He slowed as he drew near.

The light illuminated the yard of a house that stood alone among the orchards. He dismounted and laid his machine out of sight in the long grass of the dyke before he walked to a little bridge that crossed the water. A dog barked in the yard and charged for him, scattering gravel. He waited until it was almost at arm's length before he said quietly, "Here, boy," and the dog's snarls subsided into a friendly panting. He bent over it, saying, "You despicable cur," and lifted his own lip in a snarl. The dog grovelled.

A door opened at the side of the house and a man's voice called, "Who's that out there?"

"Just me." The cyclist walked forward. "Your chairman."

"Well, damn me. I wasn't expecting to see you tonight, Guy."

"Nor anyone else, I trust."

The man at the door was in his shirtsleeves, his waistcoat unbuttoned. "Always the mystery man, Guy. Sorry," he was laughing, "I mean Master. I take it you are here on official business?"

The cyclist ignored the question. "Is all clear? You have not done your duties as the club's Doorman."

"Very well, if that's the way you want it, Master." The man stepped out and peered into the

14

yard and then into the darkness beyond. Something puzzled him. "Where's your car?" he asked. "I didn't hear a car."

"Nothing to worry about, Pascoe. I left it out there on the verge. I imagine it's safe."

"Safe as bloody houses, me old son. There's no chance of mischief out here; haven't heard a car go by all evening. But come you on in and have a drink." He stood aside to let the other man enter. "I'm all on my own-io tonight."

"I am aware of that, Pascoe. That's why I'm here." The cyclist went ahead of his host into the light of the hall. He was hatless but wore a thin grey overcoat, too smart for cycling. He was neither tall nor short and, although his hair was grey, his shoulders were as square as a young man's and his voice was light and clear. All this Pascoe was familiar with, but the face never ceased to surprise him. The man's age was there. Guy March's skin was meshed with as many tiny, interlocking wrinkles as orange peel, and his eyes were puffed and very slow.

"Let me take your coat, Guy." Pascoe put out his hands to take it, but let his arms drop when March made no move.

"I would prefer it if you referred to me as the Master, if you don't mind, Pascoe. I am here on club business."

"Suits me, if that's the way you want it." Pascoe's red face had taken on a deeper shade at the rebuff, but he was also amused. He went to the

15

door of the living room and, with some ceremony, pushed it open. "And as the club is in session and I am the club's official Doorman, allow me to permit the Master to enter and inform him that all is clear and we are secure. There are no spies within earshot."

"If that is so, Doorman," March advanced to the centre of the room and turned around, "how is it that details of club business are in the possession of others?"

"I don't see how that can be true." Pascoe went towards the television he had been watching and switched it off. "But have a drink, old man … I mean Master, and why don't you sit down and take the weight off your legs?"

"No drink, thank you; and I shall stand for just a moment longer." March inclined his head politely. "But do be seated yourself."

It was an order delivered to Pascoe in his own house, and for the first time his good-natured features became disgruntled and he flung himself into his armchair, sprawling and insolent. "So what club business has been leaked, Mister Chairman?" he asked, deliberately refraining from calling the other man Master. "And why is it so important? What's got you in such a tizzy?"

March did not reply. He raised his chin, stretching the wrinkles of his neck, and his pouched eyes gazed motionless at the ceiling. He appeared to be listening to something beyond the room.

"If you think you hear something," said Pascoe,

"it's only the dog."

Far away, in the house behind the wall, the woman sat waiting with the cards in ordered rows before her. "I think the court is in session," she said softly. "Are we to commence?"

March shifted his gaze from the ceiling. "We have already begun," he said.

"Glad to hear it." Pascoe, not understanding what was meant, and not caring, lolled back in his chair. "Let's get on with it, Mister Chairman."

The soft sag in the texture of March's face did not change. "The club is aware of the studies I am making within the grounds of my house," he said, and his voice was calm.

"Yes, yes." Pascoe, seeking to regain authority on his own territory, was impatient. "We all know about your tunnel, Guy. Everyone knows it. Every single person for miles knows about the castle that used to stand in the grounds of Barbican House and the blasted tunnel that starts there and goes nowhere. I've known about it since I was a kid, so where's the secret, what's the point?"

March's voice, if anything, became softer. "Doorman," he said, "you say too much."

Pascoe, his patience completely gone, sat upright in his chair. "March," he said, "it's time we stopped all this bloody nonsense. We all know you are studying that pathetic bit of a ruin, and you have every right because it's in your grounds. So good luck to you … but what the hell is all this secrecy about? What's bothering you, March?"

March allowed silence to gather in the room before he replied. "There is the question of the Mary-Lou," he said.

"Hah!" Pascoe lay back and let his arms dangle over the sides of his chair. "The Mary-Lou. That old wives' tale! It didn't even bother me when I was a kid living out here in the fens and walking home alone at night. The Mary-Lou never came after me, to tear me apart and gnaw my bones. Come off it, March, the Mary-Lou isn't any secret. It's in all the books – every history ever written about this place goes on about the Mary-bloody-Lou."

The lids were lowered over the puffed eyes, revealing a wriggle of tiny veins, and Pascoe felt a tinge of remorse for his outburst.

"Come on, Guy, give it a rest. We all know that the old monster is a bit special to you ... but bugger it, man, it isn't your personal property."

"Doorman," the eyelids closed to a chameleon slit, "I informed the club that my researches had reached an interesting stage."

Pascoe nodded, humouring him. "That is true, Master."

"I informed the members that I am on the brink of discovering the true identity of the Mary-Lou ... and even the whereabouts of the Mary-Lou's last resting place. Great things can come of it, Doorman – unbelievable things!"

Pascoe stirred as if about to say something, but March raised a hand and silenced him.

"And all will come to naught if others know of

it." March paused, and when he resumed his voice became very soft. "The club was informed of this in direst secrecy, as you well know, Doorman – yet two days ago I heard a young man speak of this and of other matters which he could have known only through the breaking of the strictest confidence."

"Where did this happen?"

"Within the walls of our meeting place."

"You mean in the Pheasant and Trumpet?" When there was no answer, Pascoe said, "OK then, but who was this young man?"

The eyelids were raised a fraction. "I think you know."

"Do I?"

There was no movement from the man in the middle of the room, and once again Pascoe sat up straight. "Now look here, Guy, I know we have our rules…"

"One of which is that the very existence of our society should never be mentioned."

"I know all that, but that's just part of the business – to keep ourselves to ourselves. We are an exclusive little group, which is what I like about it, but even if I did let one little thing slip and some stupid youngster overheard it, what's the odds? What damage is done?"

Once more the chairman revealed the wrinkles beneath his chin as he raised his head. "It is as I thought," he told the ceiling. "The suspicion has been confirmed."

The woman paused as she played the cards. "Did I hear correctly?" she asked. "Does he plead guilty?"

"The Doorman admits the offence."

At this, Pascoe began to get to his feet. "What offence? What in blazes is going on here? You're prattling on as if I'm on trial!"

March put a hand on his shoulder. "No need to rise, Doorman. It's all over."

"Bloody glad to hear it!" Pascoe shuffled the hand from his shoulder and sank back into his chair, allowing his indignation to diminish. "God knows what you'd be like if this was a real trial, Guy, you savage old bugger." He laughed, shaking his head.

The tension had gone. March let out his breath. He smiled, and his puffy face was friendly and pathetic. He was less certain of himself. "I will have that drink now, thank you. No, don't get up – I only want coffee, and I know where you keep it."

Pascoe, a look of amusement on his face, watched him as he moved to the door of the kitchen. "As you've decided to stay, take off that damned coat, will you? And those gloves – what the hell are you doing wearing gloves indoors?"

The other man went into the kitchen without replying. There was the sound of a drawer being opened and the rattle of cutlery.

"That's the knife box," Pascoe called out. "Watch your bloody fingers, Guy." March came

20

back into the room empty-handed, and Pascoe clicked his tongue and shook his head. "Some people!" he said, in a good humour now. "Some of them don't know their arse from their elbow! Hold on, I'll make you a cup."

But March stood in front of him preventing him rising. "Look at your waistcoat," he said, and when Pascoe made himself double-chinned as he looked down, March leant forward and spread a gloved hand on his chest, saying, "Now do you see?"

"I can't see anything with your damned hand in the way."

March brought up his other hand as if to indicate the place more accurately. "Just there," he said and pointed to a spot between his spread fingers.

"What the hell!" Pascoe's face came up, mouth open in surprise, his eyes not understanding what they had seen. There had been a glint from something in March's pointing hand.

"There's a mark," said March, "just there," and he leant forward to put his weight behind the thin kitchen blade as he pressed it between Pascoe's ribs at precisely the point he had been feeling for.

Surprise widened in Pascoe's face and then, for one anguished, piercingly painful moment, shock became fear before endless darkness flooded in on him.

A red king lay alone on the table. The woman covered it with a queen and a jack. "All is as it

21

should be," she said.

March watched until a momentary quiver made one of Pascoe's knees bend and then straighten, scuffing the sole of his shoe across the carpet. Then he pulled out the knife and left, leaving the door unlocked.

He trembled and his heavy jowls quavered as he whimpered. He seemed hardly able to walk, and the dog came forward and fawned on him. March, as if he performed a kindly act, left the knife in its throat and threw its body in the dyke.

"I can't afford to leave you barking all night," he said.

CHAPTER THREE

In the private suite on the top floor of the Pheasant and Trumpet Hotel, Mrs Hogge put down the phone, closed her eyes and took a deep breath before turning to her son. "It really is too bad of you, Harry." She was a large woman, and there was a hint of armourplate in the upright neatness of her jacket and skirt. "We could do without this."

He looked at her blankly, and she said, "Anna has just told me that there is a girl waiting for you in reception."

"Must be Miranda."

"It is certainly not Miranda. Miranda is well aware that she is welcome to come up here at any time without invitation."

"I'd better go down."

Mrs Hogge had not finished. "Your father is already very busy because of this dreadful business with poor Mr Pascoe – Sergeant Thrush is with

23

him now – and on top of it all, your so-called friends have started to clutter up the foyer."

One friend was hardly a clutter, but he let it ride.

"You know very well that anyone who comes to see you must use the back stairs."

"Except Miranda."

"How such a charming girl has taken up with my son I shall never know, so let me remind you yet again we do not cater for hobbledehoys. Who is this person downstairs?"

"It's a girl, that's all I know."

"Get rid of her as soon as you can, whoever she is."

"If she's the wrong sort for the Pheasant and Trumpet," said Harry, "I'll throw her out." He closed the door on his mother's exasperation and went down.

Before he reached the foot of the stairs he could see that the foyer was empty but Anna, the receptionist, beckoned him over to her desk. "I've put her in the coffee lounge," she said.

"Thanks, Anna. Who is she?"

"Never seen her before. But you'd better be careful, young Harry, she's jumpy enough to run away. Is she your latest?"

"There's never been anyone but you, Anna." There was five years between them.

"Thrills!" she said. "When can I tell your mother about us?"

They grimaced at each other as he crossed the foyer.

At that time in the morning the only light in the coffee room came from the windows overlooking the market. Emma Judd, standing by one of the tall windows, started as he opened the door and let a magazine she was pretending to read fall to the floor. She was so hesitant that he got to it before she did and picked it up.

"Sorry," she said. "I'm very clumsy."

"I know." He smiled as he spoke, guilty about the last time they had met and not meaning to offend her, but he did not succeed. She was puzzled and worried, and he said, "I mean, I had to pick up some books you dropped in the Crescent the other day, if you remember."

She nodded, but for a long moment language deserted them. She felt out of place in the cool, dim room where the heavy curtains were swagged like clouds. He saw her touch her lips with the tip of her tongue before she suddenly plucked up courage to speak.

"I don't know what to do," she said.

"About what?"

"The man who's been murdered." He was blank, seeming not to understand, and she leant forward. "You heard me talk about it the other day in the Crescent ... the voices I heard. Mr Dorman."

"Oh, that," he said flatly.

Her eyes flared at him. "Yes, that!"

Her vehemence angered him. She was not going to make him join in her hysterical performance over something she may or may not have heard.

"But the man who was killed was called Pascoe, not Dorman," he said.

"I know that. But it's only a name! Everything else is right – you've got to see that!"

"Well," he knew that slowness would madden her, "it's true that Mr Pascoe used to come to the Pheasant quite often. That's why the police are with my father right now."

She was startled. "The police are here?"

"Sergeant Thrush. He's finding out all he can about Mr Pascoe's friends and his movements, all that stuff."

"I'll have to tell them." Her breathing had become so shallow he thought she was about to faint.

"I wouldn't if I were you."

"Why not?" She was so pale that, in spite of himself, he took pity on her.

"You know what Sergeant Thrush is like."

She shook her head.

"He'd just make you look small," said Harry. "He'd never believe you."

"You know him?"

"I've seen him around..." downing free pints behind the door of the back bar when he was on his rounds. Harry did not want to have to back up her story under the sergeant's cynical eye. Besides, she had heard nothing; he was certain of that. "I'd keep it to myself if I were you."

Her voice became calmer. "You don't believe

me," she said. "You don't believe anything. You are the same as all the rest."

Harry shrugged, but the gesture was more dismissive than he intended and suddenly she was angered. "I thought you were different. That's why I came to you. I thought you could help me."

This had happened to him before. It was something to do with being quite large, and unaggressive. He sometimes wished people would be afraid of him because of his size. They never were. "I'm not laughing at you," he said.

She did not turn towards him immediately but, when she did, her lips had a twisted smile. She waited until he nodded. "But you still think it's all nonsense. Please don't deny it – just let me take you to someone else who heard what I heard, and then see what you think!"

The market place was busy but she hurried through it and down a side street too narrow for cars. She said nothing, and he looked sideways at her. He had never paid much attention to Emma Judd. She was one of the village people who came and went at the college, always having to catch buses and never strolling through town or hanging out near the bridge or the market square when the day's work was done. Her studies never seemed to cross his, and this girl with the wild black hair and the skirt with a lopsided hem was someone he felt he had never seen. She was embarrassed to be with him, not daring to look his way, which he was glad of. It gave him a chance to see that she had a nice mouth and a small, blunt nose. But not his sort of girl; not at all. Nothing like Miranda's style; nowhere near. And on top of that she didn't like him, so why had she bothered him? It was obvious enough. He had the size to be impressive, but he was too soft to make enemies. Why else pick him out of the blue? Then she shocked him.

"I'm not trying to get off with you, if that's what you're thinking," she said, watching her toes.

"I never thought you were."

"You will after this, I expect."

"I already have a girlfriend."

"And she's beautiful, but that won't stop you."

He tried to be casual. "Who knows?"

"It won't do you any good. I've never thought of you as a boyfriend."

"Thanks."

"That's all right … just so long as you know. We're nearly there."

The Crescent was only a short walk from the market place, and she walked quickly to the archway at the centre of the curve. They went through and down a flight of shallow steps that jinked around a doctor's surgery and ended in a lane behind the houses. Trees leant over the walls of hidden gardens.

"Moat Lane," she said.

"I know."

"Because it used to be a moat when the castle was up there." She glanced up at the rooftops of

28

the Crescent.

"I know. I live here."

"I was forgetting." The grey eyes glanced at him briefly. "It's seeing you in that hotel; I keep thinking you're a visitor."

They walked in silence until the lane, turning a sharp corner, opened into what appeared to be an enclosed yard. It was no more than a place where he lane forked, but squeezed to one side was the front of a little house. Its bricks were blackened with age, and its windows were so tiny and askew and its doorway so pinched that its whole face seemed puckered with the strain of preventing the high walls on either side from collapsing on top of it. Emma pointed to a tub of flowers that stood beside the door.

"We are in her front garden," she said. She pointed to the flagstones. "And you had better wipe your feet because she scrubs all this."

"Who does?"

Emma did not answer but went up to the front door. There was a brass bell-pull, a brass door-knocker, and a brass letter-box which she could have rattled, but she ignored them all and, turning the brass handle, opened the door and went in. He followed her into a hallway that was as narrow and dark as a wardrobe. A china doorknob glinted in the gloom and she turned it.

"I'm here, Auntie," she called.

The room was dim and as cramped as a ship's cabin. Its curtains were half furled, and its

29

furniture seemed packed close so as not to shift if the deck should tilt. Something was cooking in the black oven set into the fireplace.

"Smells good," said Emma. "How are you, Auntie?"

Her aunt added extra ballast to the room. She was fat, and her bulk was supported by the struts of a high-backed wooden armchair. Her roundness meant that she had almost no lap, but on that narrow ledge sat a cat as grey and fluffy as a cloud. Emma stroked it as she leant forward to kiss her aunt's cheek. "And how is Smokey today?"

Her aunt breathed out like a puffball. "Who's that you brung in?" she asked, not looking at Harry.

Emma told her, and immediately added, "He wants to hear about the voices, Auntie."

"Oh?" The small eyes narrowed suspiciously. "You've changed your tune then, gal. The other day you was telling me it were all a load of old squit and we wasn't going to tell no one."

Emma coloured and glanced quickly at Harry. "I only said it because you live here all alone, and I didn't want you to be frightened. It's all changed now, hasn't it?"

"Because of him." She nodded towards Harry. "You've told him all about it, so now you don't care if you make your old auntie seem a fool, just because you got him in tow."

"No," said Emma. "He doesn't mean anything to me … honestly!"

"Do he know that?"

Emma's expression implored Harry to say something. "That's right," he said, "she doesn't like me at all."

Emma bit her lip. "That's not what I meant, Harry."

"Ha! Now I see how the land lies, right enough." Aunt Rose had been well named. Her round cheeks were rosy, and her lower lip was pushed forward like a pink petal. "You're in this together, the both of you, and me lips is sealed."

Something in her tone made Emma look at her carefully before she said, "You've heard something else, haven't you?"

"I shall never say no more to a person who don't treat me like I had all me faculties. Me lips is sealed as if they was put together with hot wax and stamped with the royal seal itself. Me lips shall never open no more to tell Miss Emma Judd, me own true flesh and blood niece, the best sweet girl that ever was until she took against her lonely old auntie who have no company except this great big ugly ball of fur what come off all over the furniture and is the plague of me life, bless him, but he can't talk – and no more can I."

She took a breath. "Never a word shall pass these lips of mine to tell my niece, Miss Emma Judd, how much she have hurt the feelings of her auntie by chastising her for hearing something she couldn't help – by which I mean her

Great-aunt Rose who have the gift of hearing things in the air such as is given to nobody else in the whole of this sublunary earth."

Sublunary? Harry avoided catching Emma's eye.

"Me lips is sealed. Miss Emma Judd's Auntie Rose will say no more about the voices they both on 'em heard plotting foul murder because Miss Emma Judd think she knows much better, that them voices did not exist outside of their heads and they neither of them heard nothing. The outcome of it being that both on 'em is considered as mad as the maddest hatters ever to make hats on this wicked earth."

"You've heard something else, haven't you, Auntie?"

"Jesus Christ Almighty, gal! – I've heard them plotting to dig up that there horrible Mary-Lou which I have known about all the days of me life but which I never believed existed until this moment ... and one of them's going to a secret meeting to tell all of 'em about it!"

"To tell *everyone*?"

"Everyone at the meeting, you silly child."

"A secret meeting ... but where, Auntie?"

Her aunt sniffed but, this time, *did* say nothing.

"Don't you know where it is, Auntie? Don't you know who they are?"

"I ain't saying. And don't ask me no more of your questions. The attitude of this young feller have struck me dumb." She heaved herself from her seat and went to get her dinner from the oven. They had to leave.

CHAPTER FOUR

For refreshment of all kinds Harry went to the Duke's Head. It faced the Pheasant and Trumpet with the length of the market place between, and his friend Giles Foot lived there.

Foot put down the beer tray and handed Harry a full glass. "Mild ale," he said. "Why you go for this old tack I'll never know."

"Taste," said Harry. "I've got taste. And I can't get it at home."

"One up for the Pheasant," said Foot. "My father only gets it for the scraggy old men in the corridor downstairs."

Harry always had to pass their bench on his way to the living quarters on the top floor of the Duke's Head. The old men always joked with him as if he were one of their own, which was disconcerting, but his good nature made him play up to it. "I could have asked them about the Mary-Lou," he said. "They'd treat it more seriously than you do."

Foot was small, with a sallow, smooth complexion, and his neatness was emphasized by his glasses which had perfectly circular, very thin black frames. If he ever took them off, which was rare, he seemed indecently exposed. Now, with one finger, he pushed them higher on his nose, which was a habit, and said, "Couldn't her peculiar Aunt Rose have told you?"

"It was all a bit embarrassing, Foot. We were in that tiny house and she had just told Emma that she would never speak to her ever again when she suddenly started shouting at me about the Mary-Lou! I had no idea what she was going on about."

"But you know about the Mary-Lou," said Foot.

"Of course I do. When I was a kid I was always scared to be out alone at night anywhere in the fens. The Mary-Lou used to come out of the mists and get you. But what the hell was it, Foot? All I was ever told was that it would pull you to bits and eat you."

"Isn't that enough?"

"But at least I could have asked her about it – what it was and where it got its name. Stuff like that."

"Would she know?"

"Well, she did say she'd heard her voices saying that someone had found where the Mary-Lou lay and was going to bring it back to life."

There was a pause and, in the silence, Harry at last realized that he had been treating a ridiculous matter far too seriously. He grinned at Foot, but the eyes behind the uncompromising glasses looked steadily back at him. "You have a strange mind, Hogge. You remind me of someone."

"Who?"

"If I told you, you wouldn't like it." He paused until Harry raised his eyebrows, asking the question, then he said, "You are very like that girl. The mad one who hears voices; your Emma Judd."

"She's not mine."

"But she thinks she is. That's quite obvious. Why else would she entice you to go with her to Aunt Rose's hideaway? It makes the blood run cold, Harry, to think of you being lured into that stifling little room with two mad women talking of murder."

Harry drank his beer and looked at the floor. There was something in what Foot said. Voices in the air that no one could hear; a girl who, by relying on his sympathy, had almost persuaded him to take her seriously; and then Aunt Rose's outburst. That had been one step too far. The hysteria of an old woman and a girl had made a fool of him. He raised his head. He had to put Foot right on one thing.

"You are quite wrong about Emma Judd," he said. "She doesn't mean anything to me."

"Give her time."

"Well, she'd have her work cut out. I am not going to desert Miranda, am I?" The thought made Harry very comfortable with himself. "You just don't know how much Miranda means to me, Foot. You can't know, because you just don't feel anything like it. You always stay aloof. And you never surrender to anyone."

"Of course not."

"Well, in that case you can't ever fall in love."

"I can't ever be made a fool of, if that's what you mean."

"No, what it means is that you daren't take a risk. Falling in love is taking a risk, Foot. You forget yourself and think only about someone else. You are scared to risk it."

"I see the dangers, Harry, my lad."

"And then you run away because you're a coward."

"A realist. And I know something you don't. I see both sides of falling in love, and you see only one. You believe it's sufficient to sacrifice yourself to someone else ... but what if that other person doesn't do the same?"

"You know when it happens. Everything tells you. The way the other person feels about you is just obvious. You become alive to it, Foot; you sense that something new has happened and it's wonderful."

"It must be terrific."

Harry did not respond, he knew better, and after a moment Foot said, "I am not surprised you find Miranda Merchant desirable, Hogge – so do I, as it happens, very much indeed – but I see something in her that I admire so greatly that it makes me determined to have as little to do with her as possible."

"And what's that?"

"She has a clear head."

"And that's a failing?"

"It is in a lover. She doesn't only see through you, Harry, she sees through herself."

"That's not a fault. You are just making her more attractive."

"You want an example?" He paused until Harry nodded. "Well, I should think she knows more about the Pheasant and Trumpet Hotel than you do yourself."

"If you are trying to tell me she's a gold-digger, it won't work."

"She is not gold-digging in the least. She merely sees what I see – that the Pheasant and Trumpet Hotel is part of what makes you attractive. It's part of you, Harry, and you can't get rid of it."

"That's untrue. I am what I am." But Foot had scored, and Harry felt it. He was trapped by the Pheasant and Trumpet. It marked him. He tried to escape by throwing up a smokescreen. "You are quite wrong to say she knows more about the hotel than me; she can't. She wouldn't even know how many rooms there are." It was a childish argument and Foot demolished it.

"That's no test. Not even you can tell me how many rooms there are."

"Thirty-three," said Harry, "precisely."

Foot sighed. "I didn't ask you how many bedrooms there are with numbers on the door; I wanted to know how many rooms there are altogether."

"Oh, well, twice that." Harry didn't care; he was happy to escape more questions about Miranda. "Say sixty-six," he said carelessly, but he had not reckoned on Foot's passion for precision.

"Wrong. There's more than a hundred."

"Well, I should know." Harry was as close to being indignant as his nature would allow. "I live there, and I know there can't be a hundred rooms."

"Prove it."

Harry was glad of the challenge, nonsensical though it was. It took his mind off other things, and he had no way of seeing where it would lead. If he had, he would have drawn back.

They were still arguing when they entered the hotel foyer. From her reception desk within its alcove Anna twinkled her fingers at Harry, and then he had to prevent Foot beginning the room count with the alcove itself.

"It was a room once," said Foot. "You told me it was a room until it was altered."

"This is an old place, Foot, and a lot of things have changed over the years, but I say a room is a room only when it's got a door."

"So that lavatory is a room." Foot pointed to the sign.

"I suppose so," Harry conceded, "but not every cubicle."

They were still disputing this when they climbed the staircase that would take them to the guests' rooms. "This is all new to me," said Foot. "You don't normally let me in through the front entrance."

"House rules," said Harry. "You know they've always made me use the back stairs, too." He was glad of it; he had long ago learned to keep the hotel side of his life hidden from Foot's caustic eye.

On the first landing there was a window that looked out over the rooftops behind the hotel. Below them a long roof stretched away from the back wall towards the river. Foot knew what it was. "You told me they used to keep thirty horses down there – there must be rooms in the stable block."

"Oh no." Harry would not allow it. "We haven't been a coaching inn for a hundred years, so the stables don't count."

He had turned away to continue climbing the stairs when Foot said, "Well, I didn't expect you to cheat, Hogge."

"I'm not hiding anything."

"Well, what's that?" Foot nodded towards a blind alcove at the end of the landing. "I can see a door in there."

Harry put a hand to his forehead. "I walk past it every day without noticing it. We never use it but you can count it."

Foot took a pace nearer to see a name in dim gold lettering on the door panel. "The Sally

Chamber," he read. "Who's Sally?"

"Search me. All I know is that it's a dining room."

"Just one room?"

"One single room, Foot, and there's nothing there but dust and cobwebs because it's too small to be much good for anything. It's no use trying the door because we never use it and it's kept locked."

"Is that so?" There was a benign smile on Foot's face as he inclined his head towards the dining room.

Harry followed his eyes. The door handle was turning, and a moment later the door swung silently open to reveal the room that was never used. There was no greyness of dust or cobwebs. Polished furniture glowed with a deep, rich colour in the soft light of candles, and they had a glimpse of a table laid with a white cloth on which silver gleamed. Warmth seemed to flow outwards as the man who had appeared in the doorway turned to speak with others still within the room.

"Thank you, sir," he said, backing out. "I shall see that no one disturbs you."

Voices murmured in reply, but no more than the corner of the dining table was visible before the waiter, still showing respect even though he was out of sight of anyone within the room, softly pulled the door closed.

Harry, suddenly aware of what would come next, tugged Foot by the arm to get him to turn away, but it was a wasted effort. The waiter had caught sight of them.

"Ah, so there you are, Master Harry."

The waiter smiled, but Harry winced. The head waiter's unctuous respect was a shame he had always kept hidden from Foot. "Were you looking for me, Mr Badgett?" he asked, moving away. "I expect my father wants to see me, is that it?"

"Indeed no," said Mr Badgett, "he and I are both fully occupied with the gentlemen within." He tilted his long head towards the door. "Fully occupied."

The waiter was a tall, stringy man and his face was severe until he smiled again, this time towards Foot. "Good afternoon, young sir," he said. "I know you to be the young gentleman from the Duke's Head, but I don't think we have yet had the pleasure of meeting face to face."

"Alas no," said Foot, choosing his words. "That must be because I normally use the back stairs." He carefully did not look at Harry as he added, "Master Harry insists."

"Quite so. The back stairs are a private entrance for the family." Long practice had given Mr Badgett the ability to bring a discreet yet friendly gleam to his eyes. "Master Harry has granted you the privilege."

Harry shut his eyes. All the years of smuggling Foot in without crossing the path of the head waiter had come to nothing. "We were just passing through," he said, moving away. "See you later, Mr Badgett."

But Foot was happy to remain where he was. "We were counting the rooms," he said, and the waiter bowed his head. "Do you happen to know how many there are, Mr Badgett? Master Harry seems to have no idea."

"The number of our rooms?" To watch Mr Badgett was to see his sinews at work. All his parts, from his bony wrists up to his neck and face, were manipulated towards politeness. "I am afraid that is a question that has never been put to me before today."

"The reason I ask," said Foot smoothly, "is that Master Harry has been trying to tell me that the room you have just come from doesn't exist."

"That will be one of his jokes." Mr Badgett chuckled.

"What I meant," Harry protested, "is that it's never used, isn't that so?"

"Hardly ever." Mr Badgett manoeuvred his tolerant gleam in Harry's direction. "But the Pheasant and Trumpet has a way of tripping everyone up from time to time – even myself. Only yesterday I found myself heading for a door that has long been blocked up and papered over."

"And that dining room," Harry insisted, "hasn't been used for ages ... not for years."

"At least not for a month," said Mr Badgett.

"It's got to be more than that!" Harry had seen no waiters running up and down stairs, no cleaners busy in the room afterwards. "I haven't seen any sign of it being used."

"That is perfectly understandable, Master Harry. It is a private dining room, and your father is at pains to keep it so."

"So who's in there today?" Harry was blunt, but he did not force an answer from the waiter.

"Aha." Mr Badgett shook his head. "The persons in there today are the same as a month ago, and the month before that. Just a small luncheon club." He had been standing within the shallow alcove as he spoke. He stepped out. "Now I'm afraid I must leave you young gentlemen."

"But can't you tell me who they are, Mr Badgett?"

"Discretion, sir." The waiter shook his head. "Discretion. They would not wish me to say."

"Not even to me?"

"Privacy. Your father's orders, sir." He went past them, a napkin folded over the arm of his white jacket, his shoulders slightly stooped as if he were permanently in the act of bowing as he went down the stairs and crossed the foyer.

It amused Foot to see Harry's discomfiture, and he did not spoil it for himself by saying anything.

"It's only a stupid little club." Harry tried to make light of it. "Who wants to know, anyway?"

"You do."

"But you have the same sort of confidential thing at the Duke's Head … the Buffaloes, and the Oddfellows, what's the difference?"

"They are not quite so secretive, Master Harry."

They were interrupted by Harry's mother on her

way down to make sure everything was in order for afternoon tea in the lounge. She paused, and for a moment silently regarded Foot, whom she distrusted. Then she said, "Good afternoon, Giles, how is your mother keeping?"

It was a jibe. The two women never met. There was a gulf between the hotel and the pub, and Mrs Hogge's handsome face was set in a stately smile that told him it would be kept that way.

"She is very well, thank you, Mrs Hogge."

"I caught a glimpse of her the other day, from a distance, and I thought she was putting on a little weight. Perhaps it's her work behind the bar." Mrs Hogge smiled. "She must take care. Give her my best regards, won't you." Her perfume lingered as she swept away.

Foot attacked the room count with a ferocity that made certain he won.

CHAPTER FIVE

Behind its high wall Barbican House sat in a well
of silence. When a door opened at the rear and
someone came out, the sound was furtively swallowed by the night.

Guy March stood motionless until his eyes
could pick out the dark presences of the trees gathered on the low mound that marked the castle ruin.
The grounds were his, but he listened like a thief.
Within the house only a single light burned. It was
in an upper room where a second figure sat at her
card table, also listening. Nothing stirred.

March moved towards the lawn and his boots
scraped briefly on the paved terrace before the
grass silenced his footsteps.

"There is a scent in the air tonight."

"A scent?"

"A scent of starlight," he said, "and orchards in
the far fens."

"Poor Mr Pascoe. Sweet Mr Pascoe."

46

"Dead Mr Pascoe, my dear. He adored the knife."

She caught her breath at that, and he was aware of it.

"It was a love stroke," he said, "for you."

March approached the mound. A short stretch of stone wall in its face was the only evidence of the castle keep above ground, but it was pierced by an arch leading to a passageway within the thickness of the castle foundations. March was not smartly dressed, as was normal with him. He wore overalls and he fumbled clumsily with his thick gloves before he managed to take a key from his pocket and unlock the gate that guarded the entrance. As he stepped inside, his steel-toed boots grated on the threshold.

"Is there darkness?" the woman asked softly.

"It is dark."

She played a card. "Are you a coward?"

"My terror is almost too much to bear."

"Then I am your strength." She could hear that his mouth was dry and his breath was shallow. "Is the gate closed behind you?" Her hand hovered with a card.

He gazed into the blackness ahead of him and whispered, "How can I tell what I will find? I shall leave the gate ajar."

"Lock it!"

"We do not know what lies ahead ... there is danger."

She stiffened in her seat before the card table,

but her voice became gentle, alluring. "My pleasure grows in darkness," she murmured. "Do this for me."

He turned, pulled the gate closed behind him, and locked himself in.

"The dead are with you," she said. "Pascoe is at your side." She sensed the thrill of the frightened blood thumping through his heart. "Are you prepared?"

He switched on the flashlight he carried and sent its beam to lick at the tunnel's distant shadows. "I am ready."

She concentrated on her game, blocking out his sensations. She was in need of a card to occupy a blank space. She dealt three from her hand, and three more without success, but when she put down the third triad he heard her quiet laughter.

"A king," she said. "The King of Spades." She played it. "The Digger King is in his kingdom!"

He began to move forward, and she played again. "And now the Diamond Queen is with him!"

"Are the cards true?" he asked.

"True."

He wore what was necessary for his task, the overalls, heavy boots and gloves, and now that he was deep within the tunnel and no light would escape to give a clue to any hidden watcher that he was busy underground, he put on a helmet and its lamp flooded the path ahead. "So," he said, "the Diamond Queen is with the Digger King as he enters the last stage of the quest for the Knave underground."

Once more she bent to her cards, riffling them as she searched before she played again. "A black jack!" she exclaimed. "The Knave shall be yours!"

She felt the surge of confidence that the omen gave to him, but she looked away from the card table, casting her eyes and her mind to the dimmest corner of the room so that he would not detect what she said. "Protect us from all ill consequences," she implored the darkness. "I cheat!"

The passageway sloped away ahead of him, not steeply, but as he followed it downwards the arched roof became lower and was blackened with the soot of ancient torches. Few people went beyond this point even if he allowed visitors to see the tunnel in his grounds; the roof was too dangerous. But night after night he had worked down here, and there was more to be done.

"I have reached the second gate," he said. It had rusted on its hinges and lay against the wall. "All is well."

There was no echo. His voice fell dead from his lips into the motionless air, but he imagined he sensed a movement in the atmosphere that had for centuries been held fast by the clamp of stone and earth. It was as if, ahead in the darkness, something had shifted.

He stood still. The passage stretching away ahead of him seemed to expand and contract in his wandering light like a body cavity pulsing around a surgeon's probe. His fear tingled also in the woman's veins. Her hands, no longer dealing cards, were clenched together and pressing down into her lap. "Sweet one," she said, "we are almost there."

Now there was no going back, nor did he wish to. He was near the tunnel's end. The tip of his beam picked out the clutter of fallen stone that long ago had blocked the passage. Sudden bravado gave him courage. "I am about to despoil the closure of centuries!" he cried, and his voice, mingled with laughter, stirred an echo at last and rolled away behind his back.

"Take care," she breathed.

"The Digger King is in dangerous territory, my love, but his touch is delicate. We are together."

She pressed her fists deeper into her lap.

Near the blockage the roof had been shored up with heavy timbers, but they had not prevented a more recent fall. Blocks of stone had been dislodged from the wall, and he could go no further. Some work on the walls looked recent, and more clumsy; it was his. One massive stone in particular had been eased out on crude rollers and lay in the passageway alongside the cavity from which it came.

He stooped over it, examining it carefully as if discovering it for the first time, and brought his lamp to bear on the side of the block. He rubbed the stone with his gloves and then tilted his head until the helmet lamp shone a raking light along its surface. Chisel marks on the stone showed up in relief and he crouched, leaning closer, studying one particular spot.

"It is the sign," he said softly. "It can be nothing else."

She detected uncertainty in him. "You have doubts?"

"There are deep eyes," he said, fingering the stone, "and the long muzzle of a wolf."

"You swore to me it was the sign!" There was sudden anger in her voice. "You swore to me it was the Mary-Lou!"

There was silence as he continued to examine the marks. "It is damaged." He rubbed again. "Nevertheless it is there."

"And there is more?" She was impatient. "You told me there was more."

From among the tools scattered on the ground he picked up a mason's chisel and put it to a horizontal crack near the top edge of the stone. "There is a split in the stone that is too regular to be accidental," he said.

"Yes, yes – I know!"

"It is perhaps a lid."

"The coffin! It is the coffin!"

His chisel tapped gently along the line of the crack until, finding a place where the gap was wider, he inserted the cutting edge, lifted a hammer and gave the chisel a sudden blow. The crack widened along its length. "An opening," he said. "It is certainly an opening."

"You thwart me!" she cried, her fists pressed deeper into her lap. "Open it!"

He left the chisel as a wedge and moved to the end of the stone. He inserted the tongue of a crowbar into the crack. Then he heaved down. The lid and the coffin's edge, like the lips of a clam, parted a fraction before the crowbar slipped and the stone closed.

March stood back. The face that had smiled down on Pascoe before the knife slid home was out of place beneath the helmet. The orange-peel skin gleamed with the oily sweat of the effort he was making, and confidence had drained from the puffed eyes. He was aware that his will was dwindling, but before it vanished completely he gathered himself to ram the bar home and haul again. The lid unlipped but he had not the strength to budge it further.

He struggled, his face hard with the anger that disguised his fear, and his words were forced through his teeth. "I need help!" he cried. "You must come to help me!"

"You are my protector," she said.

"I need your help!"

She stooped over her cards, and her fingers were frenziedly busy. "The cards do not permit it. I must not leave this room."

"Then damn the cards!" he shouted, and in a final spasm his arms made the stone lurch. It began to slide, moving as easily as if it were being helped from beneath, and then it tilted suddenly upwards.

The lid yawned open, and as it did so it trailed a clammy raggedness. The tattered fragments of grave clothes clung to it and, cradled within the rotting mesh, a head rose from the coffin's dark depth. It rose with the motion of someone lifting his head to look about him, and a hand to which fragments of tarnished skin still adhered also began to rise until the soft web tore silently and allowed head and hand to subside. The head came to rest with its sunken cheek on the coffin edge and gazed at him.

March did not move, but the lid had overbalanced and slid further. It hit the floor with the funeral thud of a drum that rolled back along the corridor while the empty eye sockets wept a spill of coffin dust.

CHAPTER SIX

Miranda was mercenary. It was one of her charms. Three marble steps rose from the pavement to the front entrance of the Pheasant and Trumpet Hotel, and when she pushed at the swing doors and saw the glint of the bevelled glass panes they were the facets of huge diamonds, and what lay beyond was paradise. She said so as she trod the yielding deep blue of the carpet in the foyer.

"And it's the smell!" she said to Harry. "It's a kind of warm perfume with lovely food in the background and just a tiny hint of public loo."

Harry laughed.

"It's wickedness," she said. "Knickers off ... and don't pretend you've never noticed. You'll have to marry me, Harry, and not that Emma."

"Emma?" Her frankness had caught him out. "What's she got to do with it?"

"Didn't you see what was in her mind the other day in the Crescent when she was all upset about her *voices*? She didn't want to speak to *me* ... she just wanted to cling to *you*, that was obvious."

"I didn't notice anything like that."

Miranda shook her head at him, quite cheerful at the thought of having a rival. "You love it, Harry. There's nothing you'd like better than having two of us after you. But there's one thing you mustn't forget ... I understand her because she's a girl, just like me."

He puffed out his cheeks, denying that any girl could be Miranda's equal, but she would have none of it. "She thinks she's your sort, Harry – although I doubt if she even knows she thinks it. But I do."

"What she thinks won't make any difference."

"But you're flattered, and I don't blame you. So just you be careful."

Miranda, bright with mischief, looked around the foyer. "If you married her instead of me, Harry, just think what she'd do to all this. No sense of style. It would all become dingy and bed-and-breakfasty, and there'd be weird people just like herself all over the place."

Weird people made him think suddenly of the private dining room and its secret club. "How do you know there aren't strange people here already?" he said, but she didn't ask him to explain.

"On the other hand, Harry, just think how different it would be if I lived here with you!" She was laughing at herself as well as him. She came closer, clung to his arm and whispered, "And don't forget how nice I'd be to you when we were alone."

"Nicer than Emma?"

"You are a big oaf," she said, "and you're so short-sighted." He realized she was probably not referring to the glasses he kept in his top pocket because he did not like wearing them, but she may well have been. You could never tell with Miranda. "You don't see half what's going on around you," she went on, "and you think all you've got to do is smile."

He did so now and, as with everybody, it made her smile back at him. But her mind was on something else. "What do you mean there are weird people here already?"

She had made one of her lightning changes of direction, and it gave him a chance to tease her. "I'm afraid you'll never know," he said. "We never speak about it."

"Pig!"

"I'm very sorry, Miranda." He enjoyed tormenting her. "It's simply that we have a private dining room that we don't advertise, and a certain small group of people gather there who don't want to be talked about. Sorry."

"Tell me!"

She was watching him, well aware that he could not keep a secret from her for long, when she saw his expression change. She turned in the direction he was looking and saw his father emerge from the corridor that led to his office hidden away somewhere behind the reception desk. Sure of herself, she called out across the foyer, "I absolutely agree with you, Mr Hogge!"

He had some papers in his hand and he laid them on the reception counter before he came across to them. He was a tall man, dark-haired with a small moustache, and he had an easy way with him, especially with Miranda.

"I beg your pardon, Madame?" he said, playing the hotel proprietor speaking to a guest.

"I was saying," she said, "that I absolutely agree with you."

"Oh, really?" One eyebrow was raised.

"I agree with you about your son. You are quite right to ban him from using the main entrance."

Mr Hogge's Adam's apple went up as he laughed. "He's told you about that, has he? We didn't want him trailing in here with his muddy feet when he was a grubby little urchin."

"He still is."

Mr Hogge glanced with amusement at his son before turning back to Miranda. "But the young man must have some good in him," he said. "Some of his friends are charming."

"Oh, Mr Hogge." Miranda demurely lowered her eyes, flirting with him. "But I'm afraid Harry is still very uncouth."

It pleased Harry that she charmed his father; it was her nature, but he could see what she was leading up to and it bothered him. He stirred, meaning to interrupt, but it was too late.

"I have just asked him something about the Pheasant and Trumpet Hotel, Mr Hogge, but he won't tell me what I want to know."

Harry's father raised both eyebrows. "And what would that be?"

"Well, there's a private dining room somewhere and he won't tell me who uses it." She looked directly into Mr Hogge's eyes. "He says it's a secret – but I know it can't be, now can it?"

Mr Hogge's gaze shifted to his son, and held steady. "Harry?"

Harry felt the chill of his father's expressionless face. He shrugged but it failed to disguise his uneasiness. "I saw Walter Badgett coming out of the Sally Room the other day," he said.

"So he told me." His father waited.

"I asked him a few questions."

"And you heard his answers?" Mr Hogge was brusque. There was no mistaking the change in his mood.

Harry nodded.

"Then I suggest," said Mr Hogge, "that you bear in mind what he told you and act accordingly." A telephone rang and, behind the desk, Anna picked it up but even before she had said a word, Mr Hogge called across, "That will be for me." He turned and left them.

"Oops," said Miranda. "Poor Harry – I think I've got you into trouble."

His mouth was dry and his grin could not have fooled her, but he managed to say, "That's how it goes. Hotels have to be careful." But the hurt remained.

His agitation had taken them across the foyer and out through a side door into the innyard. It was a small cobbled space into which coaches had once clattered to change horses. Old buildings still crowded around it, and Miranda, finding herself in the open, laughed. "What's wrong with you, Harry? You said you were taking me for coffee."

He flung back his head and looked at the square of sky above. "I'm at the bottom of a well and it's all your fault, Miranda. You make me forget where I'm going."

She did not reply, and when he brought his eyes down to her he saw that her attention was held by something else. In the corner of the yard there was an opening tall enough to let a stage-coach pass through and beyond it there was the stable block. It was a covered road with the stalls on either side and it was grey and bleak and empty except for a single figure sauntering towards them.

"Damn," said Harry under his breath. "I could do without this." The vehemence in his voice was unlike him and he glanced shyly at Miranda to see if she had noticed, but she was smiling at the new-comer. He came towards them, taking his time as one who was sure of a welcome wherever he went. "Great to see you, Miranda," he said, and then, as an afterthought, "Hi, Hoggy."

Donovan Brett was an athlete in a dove grey suit. He was handsome enough for a catalogue, and even his smile had muscle. "The leisured classes are on their way to partake of coffee, I suppose," he said, his eyes not leaving Miranda.

"Maybe," she said, "if you are buying." Everything may have been all over between them, but Miranda did not let that trouble her.

"Buying?" said Donovan Brett. "Me? You must think me a member of the idle rich." He had leant forward, pressing the fingers of both hands on his breast, so typically theatrical and meant to be amusing that Harry felt his lip curl. "I'm a working lad, I am."

"First time I've heard of it," said Harry. He was taking a risk because Brett's touchy temper was as well-oiled as his muscles.

"Oh, but sir," Brett's smile gleamed like a polished knuckle, "I am at work now – performing my studies at this present moment in time."

And as full of redundant words as an American film actor, thought Harry, but Miranda was amused. "You'll be getting your usual grades then, Donovan ... C minus."

"But I *am* studying. I kid you not, Miranda." His beautifully engineered head turned towards Harry. "I am at work right now, isn't that so, Hoggy?"

"If you say so." Harry, having no idea what was in Brett's mind, was indifferent.

"There you are, Miranda. This stout fellow knows all about my studies." He moved as if to put a friendly arm around Harry's shoulders, but

Harry stepped back, at which Brett said, "Oh, I'm so sorry, Hoggy. I'd forgotten I must not take liberties – not in my lowly position."

Brett was known for his disdain towards others, and the little bow he had given Harry amused Miranda. "But what are you *doing*, Donovan? You've got to tell me."

She took a step closer to him and became temptingly feminine, comically trying to wheedle something out of him. She was joking, but Harry suddenly saw them for what they were: two perfect people. They knew things that less beautiful persons could never know; they were a pair.

"Very well, Miranda, I shall tell you what I have been doing. I have been running an errand."

"Where to, Donovan?"

"That I am not at liberty to say. All I can tell you is that, in the eyes of some people, I have been a naughty boy."

"That I can believe."

"It is no joking matter, Miranda. I gave away a secret, something rather confidential, and I was sent by my employer to apologize."

"A secret! Then you must tell me, Donovan."

Brett glanced sideways at Harry before he replied. "You had better ask Mr Hogge junior. He will know. All I think I ought to tell you is that I discovered the identity of a small group of persons who dine together in this hostelry, and I said rather too much about them in another place."

Harry frowned and said, "What group are

you talking about?"

Brett merely closed his eyes.

His arrogance was too much for Harry to bear. "I know what it is!" he burst out. "It's a luncheon club, isn't that so?"

Brett tilted his head as if he were contrite and Miranda opened her mouth to say something, but when she saw the feverish humiliation in Harry's eyes she remained silent. Donovan Brett, missing none of this, went on speaking.

"I was ordered to go to the chairman of the club to apologize," he said, "and I expected a right slagging off, I can tell you … but, do you know, the lady of the house was so impressed by my demeanour that she forced me to accept this as a token of no hard feelings." He held out his arm so they could see a wrist-watch. "Expensive, I think," he said, "and that's not all; the old gentleman even wrote out a recommendation that I am to give to my employer." He took an envelope from his pocket. "There it is, Hoggy. Put your glasses on and read it if you like. No? Well I'm just about to show it to the boss as proof of mission accomplished. Shall we go in?"

His employer was obviously in the hotel, so there was no choice but to go inside with him. Miranda, taking pity on Harry, hugged his arm but he ignored her and in the foyer he stopped, expecting Brett to leave them. The foyer was empty, but Brett made no attempt to seek out whoever it was he had to see. He stood still and looked around, spreading his arms and saying, "All this ... isn't it wonderful? And don't women love it, Miranda?"

"Harry knows we do," she said. "I told him."

"Ah, women!" Brett raised his eyes. "Some of my most intense experiences have been in hotels."

"Not this one," said Harry.

"Not yet." Brett's smile was self-assured. "Give me time."

"You'll find it difficult." Harry loathed Brett's fearsome vanity. "My father can see your sort coming a mile away."

"That's rather priggish of you, Hoggy. But you have just reminded me where I must go. I have to see your father."

"What for?"

"This note, Hoggy." Brett still had it in his hand. "He wants to see it."

"What on earth for?"

"Because he's my boss ... at least in the holidays." He saw blankness in Harry's face, and his tone changed. "Didn't you know I always wanted to be in the hotel trade, Hoggy? Big ambition of mine. And your father, seeing great potential in yours truly, has taken me on as a kind of part-timer to gain a bit of work experience."

Harry was silent.

Brett regarded him for a long moment, and then said softly, "Hasn't he told you, Hoggy?"

The muscles in Harry's jaw had tightened too much for him to speak. He turned his back and walked away.

CHAPTER SEVEN

"Here!"

It was late and Harry had just come into the hotel from the side door in the innyard. It was a wet night and he was soaked.

"Here!"

A crooked finger beckoned him across the dim foyer and he moved quickly, glad of the shadows. "Hell, Hobby," he said, "you made me jump."

"Think I was your old man, did you?" Hobby Hobson, the night porter, was deeply gratified at having caused alarm, but his heavy jowls maintained a bulldog's gloomy droop.

"He's not around, is he?" It was long past midnight and Harry had hoped to get in unseen.

"He's around all right." Hobby's small eyes, black as currants, looked at him suspiciously. "That's what I was going to ask you – what's going on?" His night porter's fawn jacket with the epaulettes was buttoned up but failed to give

Hobby any dignity; he was too short, too flabby and too round-shouldered. "Something's up, and I ain't been told nothing."

"Search me." Harry was used to Hobby's attempts to wheedle information from him. "I've been out all night, and it's very late."

"It ain't late for some of us." Hobby was aggrieved. "You'll be in your comfortable warm bed in a minute, but I'll be down here, won't I?"

Harry nodded understandingly. Sympathy was always his downfall. "It must be tough," he said.

"Is it? You think it's tough?" The crumpled face was bitter. "You'd think it was a bloody holiday the way some people go on."

Harry recognized Hobby's digs at his father, but this time he did not have to respond because at that moment an outside door opened. They both stood, listening, companions in eavesdropping. Whoever it was who had entered from the innyard was still stamping his feet to shed the rain when the office door opened and they heard Harry's father say, "So here you are at last; I could have sworn I heard you a couple of minutes ago."

It had been a near thing. Harry raised his eyebrows at Hobby. They heard the newcomer, a man, murmur something in reply but the staircase prevented them seeing who it was.

"Your call sounded urgent," said Mr Hogge. "I suppose it has to be a bit more important than anything to do with the club at this time of night."

The voice was clearer. "Well now, Hogge, it is

club business in a way and I shall have something of great interest to say when we next meet ... but tonight's little item is altogether more pressing." There was the sound of a coat being shaken. "However, let's not stand here discussing it, Hogge. One doesn't want one's private affairs noised abroad."

The office door closed and they heard no more. "What did I tell you?" said Hobby. "Something's up."

Harry, unhappy with the way his father had seemed to bow to the authority of the newcomer, was moving away when Hobby held his arm. "You don't know the half," he said. "You and me ought to have a word."

"I don't see it's got anything to do with us." Harry spoke sharply, but immediately relented and changed his tone. "I wouldn't mind drying my jacket before I go upstairs. It's very wet round the neck." Hobby turned away and Harry followed him to the dark shadows behind the staircase.

The night porter had a cubby-hole, but in the middle of the night the kitchen was his domain. The door was under the staircase, and they went through into the warmth and quietness. The lines of stoves, still giving off the heat of the day, glinted softly under the light of a single lamp in one corner. Harry hung his jacket over a chair. "Is it all right if I leave it there for a while?"

"Up to you." Hobby's tone was so grudging it rekindled Harry's antagonism.

"Well, I don't want you to think I'm imposing on you, Mr Hobson."

"Mister?" The night porter's eyes darted at him, pained and suspicious. "*Mister?* Since when was I mister to you? What you doin' coming all over high and mighty as if I was nothin' more than one of your dad's employees? I thought I was a bit more than that to you, young Harry. What you trying to do – put me in me place?" His pudgy jowls quivered. "What's happened to old Hobby, then? Have he gone? Have he been given the push?"

"Oh, damn it, Hobby," said Harry, now as pained as the little man, "I didn't mean anything like that. I don't want to be in the way, that's all." Once more he made as if to leave, and once more he was made to pause when Hobby pointed to one of the kitchen's metal counters that gleamed a dull silver under the light. There were three dish covers in a row.

"Just look at that," said Hobby, and he lifted one of the covers to show a full plate of food. "That's turkey breast, that is; enough for two. And there's roast potatoes, and cranberry sauce fresh made, and all the trimmings. All done beautiful, cooked to a turn. Fit for a king, that is!"

"It looks pretty good to me." Harry was cautious, suspicious he was about to be outmanoeuvred.

"It's the pick of the leftovers, that is, and all done so nice you wouldn't think it." He lifted the other covers. "That chef, he do me proud. He think of old Hobby in the middle of the night and he do a bit extra – just you look at that sprig o' parsley there," he poked a thick finger at it, as if in distaste, "that's garnish, that is, and you don't get better service than that anywhere, no matter if you was a prince."

"Well," Harry still felt it necessary to be cagey, "you'll enjoy it … I expect."

"Delicious, ain't it?" Hobby paused to let Harry nod, then added, "And a waste of bloody good grub, if you ask me!"

"You mean you're not going to eat it?"

"Of course I'm going to eat it. I ain't that much of a fool, am I? But what time do you think this is?"

"A bit late?"

"Don't make me laugh! It's early. I don't take me dinner till the proper time, like anyone else … halfway through me work time, which is two o'clock in the morning for me. That's me proper time, halfway through me day, which is me night, if you follow me."

"I suppose that's right," Harry agreed.

"Me juices ain't ready for it until then, as your father very well know. I've told him often enough, haven't I? 'Me juices ain't on stream till then, Mr Hogge,' I told him, 'and that's when I like to eat.'" The night porter's fingers prodded the counter for emphasis. "But your dad get into such a tizzy about something tonight that he couldn't seem to stand seein' me hanging around in the foyer doing me duties. So he come up to me and say, 'Hobson, take your meal now, would you? I've got someone coming to see me and we don't want to be disturbed.' So he sends me in here to eat, and I wasn't nowhere ready for it yet, was I?"

Harry wanted to say, Well, why not wait, but he thought better of it.

"So," said Hobby, "what's going on tonight that he don't want nobody to know of? That's what I been asking meself." His quick little eyes were also asking the same question of Harry, and Harry was about to shrug when a thud from somewhere in the hotel caught their attention.

"Sounds like the outside door," said Harry. "Whoever it was he had in the office must have gone, so I'd better be getting to bed."

"That were no door." There was a smug smile on Hobby's face. He stamped the floor. "That thud came from down there. I been hearing them for months – bump, bump, bump, ever since your dad took someone down the cellars one night. They was pokin' away down there I don't know how long, and wouldn't let me down there to give them a hand or nothin'."

He waited for Harry's comment, but as it was obvious the sound had been a door closing, Harry said nothing and left Hobby to continue.

"I been telling your father about them bumps I hear in the night, but he just say that all buildings as old as this one creak a bit from time to time.

Well, if he's right, Harry, and if she creak as much as I been hearing, then she's on the move and you're going to wake up one morning and find yourself in bed in the market place, buyin' vegetables."

Harry had heard this story of thuds from the cellar many times. If Hobby Hobson was angling for an excuse to go down to investigate he could try getting the key from Harry's mother. Mrs Hogge was convinced that, until she had insisted on keeping the key upstairs, Mr Hobson had whiled away the silent hours among the wine bins. Harry risked a smile.

"You don't need to laugh, young Harry. There's something going on."

"What else does the chef leave you, Hobby? Something in a glass?"

"Pleased wi' yourself, are you? Been out havin' a good time, have you?" The night porter became slyly confidential, hinting that he, too, knew secrets. "She's worth gettin' wet for, if she's the one I think she is."

"Maybe." This time Harry was moving away, protecting Miranda from Hobby's salacious speculations.

"She done all right by you tonight, did she?"

He had listened to the night porter's silken stories of sex too often to object now. He shrugged, and a damp smile lifted the weight of Hobby's pendulous cheeks. "I reckon she must've kept her legs crossed, by the look of you."

Another thud, this time unquestionably a door, allowed Harry to escape.

The foyer was empty but the feeling that cold air had recently been let in made him sure that the outer door had been opened. The stranger must have left. There was a chance he could see who it was by looking out through the glass doors of the front entrance and he glanced that way, forgetting that the heavy outer door had been locked for the night. He missed seeing that not one, but two figures had emerged from the innyard and were crossing the rainswept square of the market place.

CHAPTER EIGHT

As Harry was climbing the stairs to his room in the Pheasant and Trumpet the two men who had left the hotel by the side door bowed their heads against the rain as they crossed the market place. They entered a side road that led behind the shopfronts to a jumble of pathways and walled yards. The rain ran sullenly in hidden gutters, and when they unlatched a gate they had to pick their way through a clutter of dripping bins and piled crates before they reached the shelter of a doorway.

One of them took a key from his pocket and fitted it quietly to the lock. "He expects us," he said softly, "but not too much noise, if you don't mind, Hogge. He likes to keep himself to himself so there's no need to advertise ourselves to the neighbours ... if there are any."

He chuckled, enjoying being surreptitious, but Harry's father raised his eyes to the grim faces of the buildings that rose above them and searched the black and dripping crevices for watchers. He was relieved when the door swung open and he was able to step out of sight.

"Stairs," his companion warned. "Steep."

Hogge was momentarily dazzled by the other man's torch. "Why don't we switch on the stairlights?" he asked.

The other man was amused. "Because there aren't any, Hogge. Once he gets up here he doesn't come down – not at night."

Their footsteps were hollow on the bare wooden treads as they climbed, and Harry's father, distrusting the echo, did his best to lessen the sound, but the other man had no such qualms. "We shan't disturb anyone now, Hogge. There's only the one tenant."

They reached the first landing and found a sharp turn that led them higher. The torch was pointed into the darkness above, and raindrops glinted on Hogge's moustache as he tilted his head. He was wet and uncomfortable, and wondered why they should be acting as though they were in a conspiracy. "It's like a warehouse," he said. "Why would anyone want to live here?"

"A quiet life." His companion resumed the climb. "You don't know my man, do you, Hogge? Not many people do, Jake's a solitary old bird."

"Well, this is no place for a sick man, and that's a fact. He should be in a hospital if he's as ill as you say."

"Couldn't agree with you more, Hogge … but try telling him that. He won't have it. That's why we've got to get him to my place, and quick."

"So you say, Guy." Harry's father was doubtful.

"Cheer up, Hogge. This is an act of charity."

On the last landing a scrap of carpet hushed their footsteps. A crack of light showed at the foot of a door and, without knocking, Guy March opened it and they entered.

Nothing stirred within the room. It was as if the single lamp that hung from the ceiling had exposed its image on a photographic plate and that nothing they saw would ever change. The lamp bulb shone within a parchment shade that threw a sepia light over a square dining table and four empty chairs. There was other sparse furniture, as brown and nondescript as the table, but the room was unexpectedly warm and beneath the plain mantelpiece a gas fire hissed industriously in the grate.

March advanced. His shoulders were hunched, and the climb had made him short of breath. "How are you feeling now, old Jake?"

His words seemed addressed to an empty room but then Hogge became gradually aware, as if time moved reluctantly here, that he was being regarded by a face reflected in the mirror above the fireplace.

"So you've got yourself out of bed, Jake. Well done." March, blinking his puffy eyes, stooped over the figure sitting in a high-backed chair before the fire. "I think you are a bit of an old faker. Here you are, fit as a fiddle, while I was telling my friend here that we'd have to dress you, you old villain." March straightened. He wore a cloth cap and the peak threw a shadow over his eyes but there was a nervous pulse to his lips that gave anxiety to his smile. He was in a hurry. "Hogge," he said, "I'd like you to meet my secretary of many a long year, Jake Hardcastle."

Harry's father took the old man's hand in his own. The skin that loosely clothed the frail bones was silky, like a baby's, and hot. "I'm pleased to meet you at last, Mr Hardcastle." A drop of rain trickled from his face and fell on the thin hand, and Jake Hardcastle started as if it had been a blow. Harry's father bent closer. "You need looking after, old chap. I think we ought to get you to hospital."

Jake's sunken face seemed too tired to be capable of any expression, but with an effort he raised his head and looked towards March. He said nothing, but the movement had asked the question for him, and his employer answered.

"Hospital?" said March. "I didn't think you liked hospital, Jake."

The old man's voice was thin and slow. "But the other gentleman thinks it's where I ought to be."

"I do think it would be for the best," said Harry's father.

March turned abruptly and walked to the window. He pulled aside the curtain and looked down into the market place. "I'm parked down there, ready to go."

There was a pause as if he was waiting for the old man to make a choice. Jake looked from one to the other, his narrow chest heaving painfully as he tried to decide which of the two men he should obey. His lips were trembling, about to speak, when Guy March broke the silence.

"Isn't that odd? I can actually see the roof of my house from here." He laughed as if it were an amusing detail, and then spoke towards it across the rooftops. "Yes, my dear, we do have a room prepared for him. And his bed is already warmed, you say? Splendid." He paused as if listening to a question and then answered, "Yes, my love, he does know all this, but he hasn't yet made up his mind."

It was a grotesque pantomime, and Harry's father spoke across it. "What are you trying to do, March? Why is it so important that he should go with you?"

March paid him no heed. He again addressed the windowpane. "Yes, he knows that the car is ready and the room is prepared..." He broke off, listening. "Yes, my dear, and he does know that you are hoping to look after him."

"March!" Harry's father cut him short. "Mr Hardcastle wants to say something." The old man had been opening and closing his thin lips.

March turned away from the window. "Tell me, Jake," he said smoothly, "do you have a tele-phone? No, of course you haven't, I know that

76

very well. But I must go out into the rain and find one because, if you have decided to go into hospital, it would be best if we asked if there is a bed for you on one of the wards. They will look after you very well, I'm sure, and – best of all for you, you old hermit – you will have lots of company."

Jake had almost given up his efforts to speak, and his head had drooped so that his chin was on his chest, but he was able to raise one hand to get his master to pause.

March was kindly. "Well, Jake, what is it?"

The old head came up and was tilted to rest on the back of the chair. "I don't want to go to hospital." He closed his eyes, panting like an exhausted dog. "If I go to hospital I'll never come out. Take me with you."

For a long moment only the hiss of the gas fire sounded in the room, and then March lifted his head and spoke to the ceiling. "We have a guest after all, my dear. You may put through that call to the doctor … yes, we shall be home before he arrives." He put a hand under Jake's elbow. "Come along, old fellow, time to go."

Guy March looked up at Harry's father. His smile was innocent, and his pitted cheeks were plump, gleaming with benevolence. "I know you don't approve, Hogge, but I'm merely being merciful. We are obeying his wish."

Harry's father watched the old man struggling to get to his feet. "He can hardly walk," he protested. "It'll take two of us to get him down the stairs ... we shall have to carry him!"

"But that's why I brought you along, Hogge. Didn't you know? Be a good fellow, would you, and take his other arm?"

CHAPTER NINE

"Anna," said Harry, wishing he didn't have to blush, "you know I'm in love with you."

"Yes, Harry darling." Anna put both elbows on the reception counter and leant forward. "What can I do for you?"

"A lot." Embarrassment made his gaze wander from her eyes, which were blue, to her neck, which was smooth. Following his direction, she tilted her head and looked down at herself.

"That's spoken for," she said. "Is there anything else?"

"I'm in trouble."

"Join the club, Harry. Your father has just been very cross with me; really nasty. I know that what happened to poor Mr Pascoe has been on his mind because he used to come here sometimes, but we hardly knew him really, so what's got into him this morning?"

"The weather." They both glanced at the miserable prospect beyond the glass doors. "And he was up very late last night."

"So I gather." She doodled with her finger on the desktop and looked sidelong at him. "Hobby Hobson told me; first thing."

"Well." He hesitated. "That's what I was going to ask you about."

"You are sweet, Harry. Especially when you lie. And I can always tell because your face crumples up a little bit just around the eyes … it makes you look older. If you could guarantee to stay like that permanently I just might weaken." She smiled. "And nothing in particular happened last night – you've got something else on your mind."

"There's a lot going on I don't understand, Anna."

"Hotels are full of secrets; you should know that."

"But nobody tells me anything, not even my father." Harry bit his lip, and then decided to speak out. "He didn't even tell me he was taking on Donovan Brett, or why."

"And you daren't ask him?" Anna closed her eyes and shook her head to prevent him denying it. "He's very touchy on that subject, is Mr Hogge … as I have been finding out this morning."

"Why?"

"Because he's come to regret it, I think. Did you know that Donovan Brett came to your father quite a long time ago and asked for a job?" Harry shook his head. "Well, he did, but your father turned him down because he doesn't like him." She looked over her shoulder. "Which is one up for Mr Hogge, although *I* don't think much of *him* at the moment, but don't tell him any of this or I'll get shot. Do you like Donovan?"

"Love him."

"Just as I thought."

"So what made my father change his mind?"

"Harry, I shouldn't be talking to you like this, behind your father's back. Where's Miranda this morning?"

He shrugged. "Gone out somewhere."

"Big break-up?"

"No."

"Pity. I was hoping to get you on the rebound."

"When you grow up a bit." They pulled a face at each other, and he said, "So how did Donovan Brett get the job?"

"You won't let up, will you? Well, all I'm going to say is that someone had a word in your father's ear, and don't ask me who it was because that's why me and your old man have had words. He thinks I said too much about a certain subject."

"A certain subject?" He looked at her so speculatively and for so long that she could not stay silent.

"Come on, Harry, you know something, too."

"Only that Donovan Brett spoke out of line about some club or other." Anna did not try to disguise that she knew what he meant. "I don't know what club it was, but he blabbed about it."

"Well, he would, wouldn't he, being Donovan. And I got the blame for telling Donovan in the first place."

"And we all know you wouldn't do a thing like that, would you?" He grinned.

"I did not! He must have found it out by snooping around where he wasn't supposed to. That's what I've just been telling your father, and he'd better believe me!"

"Keep your wool on, Anna." Harry looked around the foyer. It was empty. "I know about the club." He nodded towards the stairs. "It meets up there in the Sally Chamber. What's so special about it?"

"I wish I knew, Harry, and then I'd walk out through that door and shout it in the market place, the way I feel right now!" She sniffed. "So what's all the secrecy about? I'm not even supposed to admit that there is a club, but I know exactly when it meets because the chef knows and so does Walter Badgett."

"They are paid to keep quiet, I reckon," said Harry.

"I wish I was."

"You'll have to ask the club chairman." It was underhand, trying to get her to say something she shouldn't. Harry had become devious, and found that he could not stop. "So who runs this club, anyway?"

"After what happened this morning it's worth more than my job to say. As a matter of fact it's the one thing that Donovan Brett told me, and it's what got him into trouble." She fell silent for a moment, thinking, and then frowned and spoke quietly, as if to herself. "But now I come to think of it, there's one thing that *is* rather odd."

"What is that, Anna?"

"Those club people are so secretive it's hard to credit." She made up her mind about something and looked up. "Well, your father may not like me telling you this, but as it is something that happens when I am here but which I never see and don't know how it's done I may as well tell you. Do you know, Harry, that in all the time I spend behind this desk I have never once seen the chairman or anyone else who seems to be a member of that club come through that door and go up those stairs towards the door of the Sally Chamber. I see Walter going up and down with his tray," she nodded, "but never anyone else. So how do they get in?" The telephone rang and she turned away. "Figure that one out, if you can."

He went out. The overnight rain had stopped but clouds in the sky over the innyard were chopped by a blustery wind. It was Saturday and the bustle of the market in front of the Pheasant and Trumpet had no attraction for him so he entered the gloom of the stable block.

Anna was right, hotels always had secrets. "But I live here and they don't tell me!" His voice, echoing along the covered road, surprised him into gazing around to see who had heard. But he was alone.

From time to time it crossed Harry's mind that he did not have a proper home – a place where he could shut the door and know there was no one else in the house. A hotel was never like that. You could keep a Donovan Brett out of a house, but he could wander into the Pheasant and Trumpet at any time smirking as if he owned it. "And no one told me!" This time he let his voice roam the emptiness. Once, thirty horses had stamped the cobbles and barged the partitions of the stalls, but now only a few lifeless cars occupied the shadows. If he really wanted to be alone, he was alone now.

He walked through the shadows of the stables until he came to the road at the riverside. Traffic shuffled past heading out of town, and he had to wait for a gap before he could cross to the riverside. The brown water in its deep channel was streaked by the wind and he gazed down into the twisted ropes of water writhing as they raced out towards the sea.

The quay was deserted, and when a sheet of paper flew by on the wind, flipped over in the rush of air and settled face down on the water he barely paid it any attention. It was only when a second and a third followed the same aerial route that he raised his eyes and looked upstream.

The wind shut his eyes, and for a moment he was incapable of seeing anything but then, shielding his face with his hand, he made out the flat arch of the bridge and saw that a woman had been caught in a swirl of air and the papers had been snatched from her hands. Her coat flapped wildly and her hair swept across her face and blinded her. She was a tangled silhouette against the grey glare of the clouds and, as he watched, more papers flew free and came downstream flapping as jerkily as butterflies past the faces of the old warehouses on the far bank of the river. A few came sliding towards him and he reached for them, but the wind was jealous and laid them on the water. And then, where the river bent before reaching him, he saw one of the papers come skittering along the quay. He put his foot on it.

The woman on the bridge seemed to have regained control and hugged what remained of her documents to her breast. She was turning away but he picked up the paper and waved to attract her attention. He could not tell whether she had seen him but she remained in the middle of the bridge and he ran towards where she stooped, her back towards him, still battling the wind.

"I'm afraid it's only one sheet," he said. "I'm sorry about the rest."

"They're on their way out to sea, maybe it's the best place for them." She faced him. The woman was a girl.

"Emma!" he said. "I might have guessed."

"Why is that?" She gazed at him through strands of hair, and answered for him. "Because I'm making myself look ridiculous."

Unable to meet her eyes, he looked down at the

paper in his hand. A sentence ended at the top of the page, just two words: *among wolves*. And automatically his eye took in the beginning of the paragraph below: *A reputation for brutality had preceded Guy du Marais when he—*

Harry lifted his head. "I'm sorry, I shouldn't be reading this. Whose is it?" Another blunder.

"Mine. Why do you ask?"

Because the handwriting was not in big, girlish loops. It was very small and businesslike. "No reason," he said, covering up. "It looks interesting."

"Two months' work," she said, "and most of it going to end out on the mudbanks in the Wash for seagulls to read."

"Don't you have a copy?"

"Me?" She feigned surprise. "Don't forget I'm hopeless."

She had very small, even teeth which showed as she faced the wind and had to draw back her lips in order to breathe. She seemed again in danger of losing what remained of her papers and he put out a hand to help and then, too embarrassed to touch her, drew back. She saw what had happened, and dipped her eyes.

"Can I help?" he asked.

"Not unless you know more about the history of this place than I do." The grey eyes looked sideways at him.

"I don't know much."

"You've lived here all your life."

"I don't remember wolves." She was puzzled, so he added, "That page I looked at seemed to be about wolves."

She laughed. She had a small face, and the wind had reddened her cheeks. "Don't believe everything you read," she said.

"Especially if it's by someone who thinks she's hopeless."

She bit her lip, debating within herself, before she let him know what was on her mind. "I'm mad ... I really think I am, because I'm not writing about wolves at all ... I'm writing about the Mary-Lou. All the time, Harry ... all the time!"

"No." He shook his head. "You are writing about the town; that's what you are studying, isn't it?" He knew it was her project. "The Mary-Lou is part of what happened, that's all."

"You're making excuses for me. I'm mad." She nodded down at the pages she was clutching. "All this was meant to be the history of this place, but I only got as far as the building of the castle when it turned into something else. I just can't get the Mary-Lou out of my mind. I can't write about anything without it coming in and taking over! I'm losing my mind, I do believe."

He thought about her voices, and the old aunt in Moat Lane, and he tried to take her mind away from it. "There was nothing about the Mary-Lou, whatever it is, in that page you just let me see."

She glanced down at the sheet. "You're wrong, Harry. It's all about the Mary-Lou." Her voice was quiet but desperate. "Look at this," she pointed to the passage he had read about Guy du Marais and his reputation for cruelty, "you know who he was?" Harry shook his head. "He was the first Constable of the castle when it was built by the Normans. He had to keep all the fen people in the marshes around here under control. That's how he got his name, you know that."

She glanced up quickly and saw that he was ignorant.

"Guy du Marais," she repeated, trying to disguise her impatience. "*Marais* is the French word for marsh. It must have been a nickname to begin with but it stuck, and it got passed on to his servant, the one who tortured people and killed them – the Mary-Lou."

"I see."

"No you don't." She had seen that he was still puzzled, and there was the slightest gleam of amusement in her face at catching him out. "Do you want me to tell you?"

"Yes please, Miss." She coloured slightly, aware that he was mocking, but their eyes met and held. His own smile faded. "You can't tell anyone else," he said. "No one would listen to you."

She did not look at him. "The Constable had a special person in his castle to torture people. He called the torturer his Wolf and from time to time he'd set him loose to go and find his enemies out in the marshes. But he was a French wolf, Harry, a *loup* — and he roamed the *marais*. So out in the fens they joined the two words up and called him the *Marais Loup*."

The Mary-Lou. Neither of them said it aloud.

"Did you discover this?" he asked.

"My aunt knew about it."

They walked together from the bridge.

"Goodbye, Harry."

"Where are you going?"

"I've got to rewrite all those pages I lost."

"I'll help you."

"You'll go mad. Like me."

"I'll risk it," he said.

CHAPTER TEN

The doctor came to Barbican House and signed the certificate, and later that day the undertaker arrived to take away the body of Jake Hardcastle.

"I would like him to rest here until the funeral," said Guy March. "He was an old friend."

"Quite. Quite." The undertaker was eager to please. "That can be arranged. Certainly. Certainly. And we have taken your requirements as to the casket."

"A simple lid."

"A simple but dignified casket, the Farewell model. And you have chosen four handles in classic Victorian brass, the Awaken set." He closed the pages of the brochure. "Good. Very good. Our old friend would have approved, I am sure."

"And delivery?" March took off the small gold-rimmed glasses he had worn for studying the brochure.

"Speed is of the essence, Mr March. We could

have the late Jake boxed up very soon." Embarrassment tinged his cheeks. "Excuse the expression, Guy, it's a term we use in the trade; no disrespect intended to our old friend."

"*My* old friend," said March, "you never met him. But Jake Hardcastle kept his files tidy; he would not object to being *boxed up*." He smiled and the undertaker, confused at having been corrected and forgiven at the same instant, smiled back. "So," continued March affably, "when you say *early* delivery, how early would that be?"

The undertaker, more than ever keen to please his client, frowned and puffed out his cheeks and then spoke as if making a great concession. "What would you say to tomorrow afternoon?" He looked anxiously at the man who leant comfortably back in his chair with one elbow on the table. March closed his eyes. The undertaker was alarmed. "I could perhaps manage the morning."

March opened his eyes. "Tell me," he said, "are your coffins made to measure or off the peg?" When the undertaker began to splutter he laughed. "I want nothing but the best for old Jake, but if you must cut a corner I am sure he would not hold it against you. Could you possibly manage this evening?"

"Maybe, maybe." The undertaker was flustered. "We have our ways in the trade. We are ready for emergencies, and in your case, Guy, because of our connections elsewhere, if you understand me, we can grant you certain priorities."

"Ah," said March, "because of the club."

"Quite. Quite."

"Which reminds me," March became solemn, "our little society has also suffered a dreadful loss recently."

"Indeed we have!" The undertaker shook his head. "Who could have done such a dreadful thing to poor Pascoe? Are the police any nearer to making an arrest?"

"I shall do my best to find out before our next meeting, but I am led to believe they have very little to go on, alas," March sighed. "Meanwhile we shall have to struggle to carry on without a Time-keeper, unless ..." March kept his eyes on the undertaker "... unless you would care to be our new Timekeeper? I would appreciate as a right-hand man someone who understands so well the timing of exits and entrances." Amusement seemed to twinkle somewhere in the depths of the pouched eyes, and the undertaker sought to match it in his own as March added, "And as it happens I have a ceremonial request to make to you, Mr Timekeeper, as a member of our brotherhood."

"State it, Master, and it shall be done."

"It is a question of a Lying in State."

"For our ..." the undertaker inclined his head "for *your* old friend?"

"Jake Hardcastle was never one of us, Mr Time-keeper, but he knew of my studies ..." he pursed his lips "... my researches underground."

"He kept your records, I believe."

"He kept my records and was well aware of how close we are to achieving our end so, in order that he may share it in some sense, I would like him, for tonight at least, to rest within the tunnel itself." He paused, and when the undertaker did not immediately reply, he added, "Is there some difficulty?"

The undertaker cleared his throat. "It is unusual."

"It will be between ourselves."

"It is *very* unusual."

"No one but ourselves will know. There is a gate to the tunnel and it shall be locked. I wish to keep vigil over the remains of my old friend."

"In that case..." The undertaker's face brightened and he rose from his seat, suddenly businesslike. "One of my men has been with me a long time. He will do as I say without question. You can rest assured that we shall perform this final duty for the old gentleman. Yes. Quite."

"Good man." March was also businesslike. "We shall meet at dusk, if that suits you? Good." He put a hand on the undertaker's shoulder and became confidential. There was a chuckle in his voice. "The lady upstairs also thanks you. We were faced with the prospect of taking old Jake out there by ourselves tonight, and I have told you how reluctant she is to leave the house."

"Oh dear, oh dear. He was quite a big man and she is a frail lady, I have heard you say; you could hardly have managed it."

"Exactly, Mr Timekeeper. I was relying on you."

Guy March showed the undertaker out and then climbed the stairs to the room where the dead man lay. He entered quietly and stood for a moment looking at the shape on the bed, its contours barely visible beneath a white sheet.

"Purity," he said softly. "Dressed like a bride."

The faint riffle and flutter of cards being shuffled and dealt made him raise his eyes to where she sat at her table. "Dusk, my dear," he said.

Flutter and tap the cards went down. "And the lid?" Her voice was as soft as moth wings. "Will the coffin lid be a problem for you?"

"Wood is much lighter than stone, my love."

"Ah." Her hands were stilled.

When the light had almost left the day, and the walled garden was blurred with grey, the coffin swayed between two men across the lawn and into the tunnel's mouth. They were familiar with tombs, but the blank darkness ahead of them was questionable and they were relieved when the man who waited for them told them to go no further.

"The roof is dangerous beyond this point," he said.

The men placed their load on two trestles that March had got ready for them, and he locked the gate. "I shall return to keep watch until dawn," he said.

The two men were back in the hearse that had brought the coffin before they spoke again. "He's a brave man is Mr March," said the undertaker and answered himself, "yes, he certainly is."

"Not the sort of job for me," said his companion.

"But mum's the word, Joe, don't forget."

"Don't you fret, I'm as silent as the grave." Their laughter was muted by the purr of the motor as they pulled away.

The greyness of the dusk had darkened into definite night before Guy March left the house, softly closed the door behind him and crossed the lawn to begin his vigil. The card player had abandoned her table and lay on the bed that had, a few hours before, borne the weight of Jake Hardcastle's corpse. The only light filtered in from the lamps in the Crescent and made a spidery pattern of tree branches on the ceiling.

She felt the fibres of the darkness tugging at her and she said, "You are at the gate."

He turned the key and entered. There was silence in the room as she listened.

"Click," she murmured, "I await the click."

He locked himself in.

"You are silent." There was suspicion in her voice. "Why do you say nothing?"

"I am listening." Ahead of him the long darkness of the tunnel reached out and put its fingers around him. The hairs at the nape of his neck felt the touch and he let out his breath. His sigh came slithering back at him along the tunnel.

She sensed the leap of fear in him and spoke

softly. "There is no need to tremble like a child," she murmured. "I am with you."

The light he carried picked out the coffin on its trestles. His own panting seemed to be matched by a sound from inside, and he held his breath for pounding seconds, listening again. What if he isn't dead? The thought formed in his mind and he imagined Jake Hardcastle stir like a huge maggot in his burial clothes.

"The lid!"

Her voice jerked at him and he placed his lamp on the seat that had been placed for his vigil by the coffin. He reached to his pocket for the tools he would need, and then from an inner pocket he took a flask and drank. He paused and drank again. "Ah," he said, as the drink ran in his veins and gave him courage, "now I can see what is on the menu for tonight."

In the room, she smiled. He was himself again.

"A simple lid," he said, "for the Farewell casket. Just eight little ... ah, no, I tell a lie ... there are eight screws of substantial length." He busied himself with undoing them, taking care not to mark the polished wood, and when he had all eight gathered on top he collected them carefully and put them on the seat.

He moved to raise the lid but it would not budge. He took a screwdriver to prise it free. "It is sealed," he said. "There is a substance holding it!" Panic made him gasp, but gradually the lid came unstuck and he laid it to one side.

She spoke to the ceiling of her room. "What do you see?"

The corpse within the quilted casket was covered. "I brought no gloves!" he cried.

"You need none!"

He reached and turned back the folded sheet. An odour like long-dead flowers came with it as he revealed the dead face.

"Good evening, Jake," he said.

"What do you see!"

March looked down at the corpse, and before he replied he lifted the flask to his lips. "He does not look comfortable," he said. There was a distasteful grimace on the dead face.

"Do what you must!"

"My poor old friend." March was not drunk, but gave himself courage by pretending to be so. "Give me your hand, Jake."

He reached into the coffin and lifted the skinny arm and hand.

"Knife," he said. "Where's my little knifey?" It was on the seat. "Your fingers are cold, Jake," he complained as he reached for it. "Just hang on, old chap, this won't take a moment."

The fingers, stiff but seeming to respond to his movements, bent slightly around his own. They curled tighter as the shining steel of his knife made inroads on the wrist and snicked through the tendons that gleamed as white as the strings in a chicken leg.

She trembled as she lay on the bed, clasping her

wrist, feeling as he cut. "Deeper!" she moaned. "Deeper!"

The fingers loosened as he sawed and, when the stump of the arm fell free, the hand was a packet of bones within his own hand.

"What next?" Her voice in his ear was quiet, submissive. "Dare you go further?"

He held the hand that had no arm and raised it. "There is nothing I dare not do!"

"I am with you in the dark, my love. Go now!"

He picked up his torch and went into the wormhole that burrowed beneath the town. "My ancestors have trodden this path," he said. He was worthy of them, and the drink had at last made him light-hearted. "The servant of my ancestors awaits me."

Layer after layer of darkness folded behind him, and when his light beam danced ahead to the stone coffin it rested there and glowed stronger as he approached. The mess of bones and grave dust lay as he had left them, and the skull gaped, gazing at nothing. He bent close.

"Wolf," he whispered. "It is time to rise."

The indifferent head, full of sightless centuries, kept its secrets to itself.

"I bring you food." He raised the severed hand above the coffin's edge and held it where it could be seen.

The dried and sunken head had no life in it.

"Food." He shook the hand so that its fingers writhed.

"Food." He moved the hand closer.

"Fresh meat." He lowered it until the dampness of the wrist touched the bared teeth.

His cry made her start upright on the bed. She saw what he saw. A tongue like a dry slug had issued from between the teeth and licked the moisture on what had been its lips.

"Stand still!" Her voice penetrated every room of the empty house. "He must see you!"

March had his back to the wall. The hand was with the Mary-Lou, held between its teeth as it lifted its head and saw him. Two shrivelled grey hands came up to grasp the pale fingers. Teeth grated on a bone, and the head tilted sideways, gnawing. March slid his back against the wall. It watched him as it ate.

He slid further and it crouched within its stone bed, still eating. He turned and ran.

"Stand still!" she screamed. "You are its master!"

It was too late. Panic winged him. His light beam stabbed the walls and the tunnel roared in his ears with the rush of his flight, but behind him, with the soft scrape of horny feet, his servant followed. He ran full tilt at the locked gate, wrenching it, too dazzled with terror to turn the key, and his mouth yawned wide as he waited to be grasped.

But no touch came. The iron bars bit into his grip until he felt blood on his fingers. Fraction by fraction he turned his head until he looked over his shoulder.

It had reached the coffin of Jake Hardcastle. The grey tatters of its garments shifted to the jerky movements of the bones beneath as it stooped over the wooden box, and its head dipped greedily into its trough.

He watched, and from time to time the head was raised to gaze back at him, grinning as it fed.

CHAPTER ELEVEN

The glittering frame of the cycle rocked from side to side as the cyclist, who was soon to die, stood on the pedals and drove it to the top of the hill.

Donovan Brett had long ago made a deal with Death. If he kept out of Death's territory, never visiting a sick room, never setting foot in a graveyard, refusing even to speak Death's name, then Death would never come tiptoeing from behind to lay a hand on his shoulder. But this morning he had breached the rule.

Harry Hogge's stupid father had forced him to ask after some old invalid in the big house in the Crescent, and he had had to return with the message that the old fool had died the day before. He had been tricked into becoming Death's Messenger, and now, in the sharp air miles out of town, he was sweating the taint of it from his soul.

And the rain came to help wash it clear. He reached the top of the hill and sat upright in the saddle, raising his arms and allowing the rain to cool his face and slick the skin-tight racing strip over his chest and along his thighs.

"Yee-har!" he yelled to the sky.

He coasted to a stop and filled his lungs with the high air. He had put the flat fens behind him, and the hump of the hill was only one of many in the new landscape. He was alone on the gritty, narrow road where there was so little traffic that grass grew down the middle. He surveyed it all.

"Nothing," he said. "Beautiful, lousy, bloody nothing!"

In a lane where no car could reach, a couple toiled up a steep slope. The rain had set in after they started walking and she accepted his jacket when he placed it over her shoulders. Harry's shirt was soon wet but he made light of it.

"It's warm," he said. "Just a summer shower."

"But look," Miranda pointed to the ground, "there's already a stream." A tiny rivulet tickled the stones in the centre of the track. "And there'll be frogs," she said. "There's bound to be frogs!"

Her dislike of frogs pleased him. He was happy to be with a girl who allowed him to get wet for her sake and was afraid of frogs. Emma would never come to him for protection, but Miranda's demands were a kind of flattery.

"Harry," she said, "stand still a moment. I need you." She put a hand on his shoulder to steady herself as she took off a sandal. The lane was green-roofed and he stood still in the mossy light and watched her shake out a pebble.

"You could walk barefoot," he said.

"You're joking."

As she straightened he leant towards her, but she pushed him away. "I can't kiss you in this horrible muddy place, Harry." She smiled at him. "Take me somewhere nicer."

At the crest of the slope the lane emerged from the trees and petered out. They stood at the edge of a meadow and looked out over a landscape that lay in soft green folds receiving the rain. Their car was on the other side of the valley and they would have to go out into the open to reach it. She shuddered in the chill, and he put his arm around her.

"You are wet," she told him. He thought the fact that his shirt clung to his chest deserved a comment, but she said, "Just look at my hair … it's all rats' tails."

Not every girl with her cheeks streaked with wet hair would draw attention to it. But Miranda's face, simplified by the rain, was freshly beautiful.

"You are as wet as a new-born calf," he said.

"That's revolting!" But she allowed him closer.

He kissed her. The rain mingled on their lips, and he felt the warmth beneath the chill of her skin. "You are so drenched, Miranda, that you wouldn't be any different without any clothes at all."

"Oh, wouldn't I?" She pressed herself against him.

"No one would see."

She said nothing.

"You'd be beautiful in the rain ... alone and pale, like a statue in a fountain."

"What a mind you've got." But she was not displeased.

"There is more in my mind than that. You've no idea what I think."

"I know exactly what's on your mind." She allowed him to kiss her again. "And it's wicked."

"But do you like it?"

"Maybe." She turned her head to look down the slope of the meadow. "I can see someone."

He saw nothing until she pointed and then, on the far side of the valley where an uneven hedge made a broken line across the face of the slope, something was moving.

"It's only a cyclist," he said, "and he can't see us. He's more than half a mile away."

Donovan Brett had slowed. He had been sent to a house where a dead man lay, and all the miles he had ridden had not put it entirely behind him. Disgust swept over him as he recalled the manner in which the news had been given him.

His foot slid out of his toe clip as he shrank away from the thought of Guy March's arm around his shoulder and the murmur, "Sad news, dear boy."

Brett swore and kicked his foot back into the clip. He gained speed, crouching low, concentrating

104

on the sight of the glittering wheel beneath him as it surfed the wet grit of the road. This was how he should be; Donovan Brett at his best, nothing but shoulder, arm and thigh.

"Who is it?" Miranda had to hold a hand to her eyes to peer through the rain.

"What does it matter? He's not interested in us." Harry used a finger to follow a line of hair down her cheek. Blonde became darker when it was wet.

Miranda shivered. "You're making the rain run down my back."

"That was the idea."

She stood back half a pace. "I'm sure I know who it is out there."

They were far from anyone they were likely to know, but she insisted that Harry should again look across the valley to where the cyclist was still cutting diagonally down the slope. "He's fast," she said. The cyclist's yellow jersey flickered through the gaps in the hedge. "He must be brave."

"Or mad." Harry narrowed his eyes at the distant, speeding figure and his expression changed. "I'd go for mad."

"You know him?"

"I know a yellow jersey when I see one. Donovan Brett." It irked him that when she heard the name she thrust her face into the rain determined to make out the flying figure.

* * *

Brett clenched his fists on the bullhorns of his machine and arrowed into the rain. He was at his best and knew it. He was designed to perform. A girl should see him now, glistening, a conqueror. His fears peeled away, and he shifted his grip and sat upright.

"He's just punched the air," said Miranda.

"Cowboys do when they shout yee-har. He probably thinks he's got an audience."

"You said he couldn't see us."

"Do you think that matters to Donovan Brett? He always has an audience."

She had kept her eyes on the yellow jersey. "He's gone into the trees. I've lost him." There was regret in her voice.

"Do you think he can have broken his neck?"

"That's mean, Harry," she said.

A stream crossed the road ahead of Brett. Training runs had often taken him this way and he knew that the ford was shallow enough to ride through. This time it was a mistake. Rainwater had swollen the stream and it was just deep enough to bring him to a stop with one foot in the current.

He swore. At least there was no one to laugh at him here among the trees, but he could not prevent himself looking around to be sure. A few yards upstream a fence crossed the brook to prevent cattle straying from the hillside and there was a stile at the water's edge, but it had rotted and was broken. It was evidence that no one had passed this way in a long time, and suddenly he did not want to be alone. He dismounted and was about to lift his machine to his shoulder when the strap of his wrist-watch stung his skin. He rubbed at it, angry that the need to scratch at his arm had left him standing with icy water curling around his ankles as if determined to hold him there.

"To hell with it!"

His voice was an alien sound under the canopy of trees where the stream chuckled to itself. The watch burned his wrist and he tried to tear it off, but his fingers were too numb so he ceased pulling at it and stooped to lift his machine. His eye caught a movement upstream. He had the impression that someone had climbed the stile, but after a moment he was certain there was no one there. He stood still and let out his breath. The movement was nothing more than a branch dipping as it trailed in the current. Nevertheless it had made him nervous and he splashed forward with too much haste so that he lost his footing on the stream bed and turned an ankle. He staggered and found himself facing the stile once more. It was as though the stream itself was forcing him to take another look.

The uprights of the stile, black with rot, had collapsed and what remained of it leant together awkwardly. The shape it made was vaguely human, but now that he looked at it squarely he saw that its head was no more than a blunt post, its hunched shoulders were a broken rail, and its limbs were old wood encrusted with fungus and slime.

He shifted his cycle to a more comfortable spot on his shoulder and began to pick his way to the edge of the stream, taking his time now that he had conquered his panic.

"He's a long time in those trees," said Miranda. "Do you think he's all right?"

"Who cares? I'd rather think about you."

"What about me?"

"I like the way your face shines."

"That's because it's soaking wet and cold."

"I was wondering if you were like that all over."

She smiled. "And you'll never know."

"That's because you are more interested in Donovan Brett."

She went close. "I think you are jealous," she said.

"But you don't deny it."

"Do I have to?" She put her lips to his to prevent him answering, but she did not prevent his mind seeing once more the confident lust in Donovan Brett's face when he had looked at her.

At the edge of the stream Brett stamped his feet to shed water from his shoes, and at the same time he gave the stile a last casual glance. Two eyes gazed back at him. No, not eyes, just the glaucous glint of two small pockets of water held by the rotting woodwork. Anxiety drained from his face and he grinned.

He was still grinning when the post lifted itself slowly upright, and the two gleaming points of liquid rose with it. They watched him.

The shape of the smile remained on Donovan Brett's face but now his lips were curled with fear. Clumsily, looking over his shoulders as he trod the pedals, he fled.

"There he is again," said Harry. "Wonder boy returns. No need for you to worry."

The cyclist, emerging from the trees, was leaning over the handlebars like a jockey on a horse's neck. But there was something ungainly about the effort he was putting into it, hauling jerkily at the machine as if it would not obey his need for speed.

"He's in a panic," said Harry.

Miranda began to walk. "He just wants to get home out of the rain – like us, if we've got any sense."

Harry did not answer. The road behind Donovan Brett was empty, but something had emerged from the clump of trees and was tracking through the fields, keeping level with the road. Harry pointed. "What's that?"

She was too late. Whatever it was he had seen had vanished behind the scanty hedge.

"Something's chasing him." Harry held Miranda's elbow. "Watch." He was still speaking when an ungainly, long-legged creature loped rapidly past a gap. "What on earth is it?"

"I don't know, Harry." She was impatient to get

home. "A sheep?"

"Much too tall. It's more like a man."

Yet no man could run as fast as the creature was travelling – and at the next gap it was even less manlike because it crouched as if it ran on all fours.

"Let's go, Harry." Miranda shuddered, hugging herself. "Whatever it is I don't like it."

"Nor does he." Donovan Brett was twisting as he rode, looking always backwards along the road. "But he can't see it – he's not looking in the right place." Harry had raised his voice, alarmed at what was happening. Now he shouted, hopelessly trying to make his voice carry across the valley. "Brett, you fool – it's behind the hedge!"

Brett was too far away to hear the cry. A different sound held his attention. It was not the swish of his tyres along the road nor the heave of the breath in his chest. It was like the silvery rustle of a breeze through grass. It came swiftly from somewhere behind, caught up with him, and then kept level. Now it seemed to come from behind the hedge and he darted a glance to one side where the hedge was thin, but he saw nothing. And then the breeze seemed to overtake him and fade.

As the sound died, the rain for a moment ceased to swirl on the hillside and he coasted, listening. And then, thank God, there was a sign that other people were near. Ahead of him, under the shelter of a tree, a car was parked.

He drew level with it and stopped. The sky was shutting down into deeper shadows as the rain

110

came again, and the car was heavily shaded by the branches. He dismounted and wheeled his machine closer. It was impossible to see if anyone was inside so he stooped to the window, smiling.

"Hello," he said, wiping the rain from his face. "Nice day."

Harry and Miranda were so drenched when they came to the ford where Donovan Brett had carried his cycle that they made no effort to find the stepping-stones upstream but splashed their way through the current. When they reached Harry's car he saw that parking under a tree had not kept it any drier and he swept his hand across the glass to clear the windscreen.

"Never mind about that." Miranda hunched her shoulders under his coat. "Let me get inside."

He unlocked the door, still looking at the windscreen. "I can't imagine where all this rust has suddenly come from." His car was old but not so dilapidated that rust would run from the roof to streak the glass. He stooped to clean his fingers on the grass when a spot of rust fell on the back of his hand and made him look up to see where it came from. It was not from the car. It had fallen from the tree, and must have been pollen or resin washed down by the rain.

But it was neither. He saw a yellow fertilizer sack that at some time had been carried by the wind to the high branches. Some chemical it had contained had coloured the rain.

"I didn't choose the best place to park," he said as the sack released a trickle that fell on his hand. But this time the drops were faintly warm. And red.

He stepped away and looked up. The trickle had not come from a fertiliser sack. It was a yellow jersey, and blood trickled from it and along a thigh before it fell from Donovan Brett's knee. Harry shouted up to him, but Brett sagged motionless, jammed in the fork of two high branches. Even before he climbed up, Harry knew that Donovan Brett was dead.

CHAPTER TWELVE

The inquest was a long time coming, and it was late autumn before Harry was called to attend. He had a troubled night. It was a matter of honesty. He did not fear having to go through his discovery of Donovan Brett's body yet again – he seemed to have talked of nothing else since he had climbed the tree and found that it was too late to do anything for Brett – what troubled him was the question of what he was to do at the opening of his evidence. It would test his courage.

The upstairs room in the courthouse was crowded. There were tables and some rows of chairs, but there was nothing resembling a witness box.

When Harry's name was called he went, as others had done, to the lectern in the centre of the room in front of the coroner's table. On the lectern there was a small black volume, but Harry lifted his eyes to look beyond the crowded seats to the tall windows overlooking the river. He could see the curve of the river below and people walking in sunshine along the quay. They seemed unconcerned, but surely they must be aware of the turmoil he was in.

"Take the Testament in your right hand, and read the oath from the card."

They were the words he had expected, but he hardly heard them. They had kept him awake in the night, thinking of himself when he should have thought of Donovan Brett. Automatically he took his spectacles from his top pocket and put them on.

"Take the Testament in your right hand."

Donovan Brett was the one who should have been here. It was his inquest … but he was somewhere else … in an ice cupboard … stony still … in the dark. But the Testament. That was the test.

"Take the book in your right hand." The coroner's officer was a policeman, but hatless as if at his ease in someone's house, and he had picked up the little black book with the worn cover and was handing it to Harry.

The coroner, believing that a schoolfriend of the dead boy needed encouragement, said, "Take the book and repeat after me…"

Harry's fingers began to straighten as if to reach for the Testament, but he suddenly curled them into his palm and pressed his clenched fist into the lectern.

"I don't believe in God."

His breath caught in his throat. It was the test

he had set himself; confirmation in public of what he believed. He had done it, but it was suddenly trivial. And there would be trouble. For nothing. He should have kept his beliefs to himself. Faces gazed fixedly at him, but only on the front row was there any movement. A hand in a black glove rose to cover a pair of tearful eyes.

And there was no trouble. The coroner was unperturbed. "Very well, officer, let the witness affirm," and a few moments later Harry had sworn, not by Almighty God but on his own honour, to tell the truth.

When he answered the first question he lied.

It was as hot as a summer's day, and the venetian blinds distributed the sunshine in slanting stripes that made faces anonymous, but when the black-gloved hand was suddenly lowered it showed eyes that were filled with anger. Donovan Brett's mother hated him. Harry Hogge was alive, and her son was dead. She blamed him for daring to mar this moment with his feeble opinions, and the spite she flashed towards him filled him with shame, and at the same instant kindled a sudden ferocious dislike in him for her and her son.

"The tragic young man Donovan Brett was a friend of yours?" the coroner asked.

"Yes, we were very friendly." It was hypocrisy, and Mrs Brett would see through it. "Everyone liked Donovan," he said.

"So it must have been doubly distressing for you when you eventually discovered who it was who was caught in the branches of the tree."

"Yes." But also something else, almost triumph. He had to dip his head because he feared what his face would show.

From time to time the coroner wrote with a fountain pen on the papers in front of him in what Harry could see was very small handwriting, and he always read through what he had written before he raised his head. He surfaced from one of these interludes.

"Now, Harry, I shall put to you a few questions and I would like you to tell me in your own words exactly what you saw." His face wore a faint smile intended to put Harry at his ease.

"Did you see Donovan climb the tree?"

"No. We were too far away."

"And he would have been hidden from you?"

"Yes."

"You did not see him until you were actually under the tree?"

"I didn't know he was there until I looked up."

"What caused you to look up?"

Harry narrowed his eyes in the slanting sunbeams. He made it a wall between himself and Mrs Brett. She had every right to hate him. He had hurt her; now he was about to hurt her again. The coroner prompted him.

"Was it something on your car that caused you to look up?"

Harry nodded.

"Does that mean yes?"

"Yes."

"And was it blood?"

"Yes."

"And when you climbed up to him what did you see?"

"He was wedged between the branches."

"And it was plain he had been wounded?"

Once again Harry nodded but this time the coroner let it go by and said, "Although this may be a difficult question for you to answer, I am obliged to ask what it was that caused you to know he was badly hurt."

"He had fallen on a branch."

"What kind of branch?"

"It was broken."

"A jagged branch?"

"Yes. It was a sort of spike."

"A sort of spike." The coroner wrote the words as he spoke. "You saw this spike?"

"I did."

"And what was the nature of the injury it had caused to your friend?"

"It had gone right through him."

There was a muffled sob so wracked with pain that no head was turned towards it. The coroner paused, leafing through papers on his table, and then said, "Everyone appreciates the harrowing nature of this evidence, but it is important that we ascertain as far as possible the events leading up to the tragic discovery."

From the corner of his eye Harry saw that

Donovan Brett's parents had clasped hands and Mr Brett's knuckles were white against his wife's black gloves. They were helpless, and pity made him despise the coroner whose relentless questions were forcing him to hurt them even more.

"You have said in your statement to the police that the deceased ..." the coroner cleared his throat and became less formal "... that Donovan was seen by you to be cycling at some speed along the lane a few minutes before your tragic discovery?"

"Yes."

"What opinion, if any, did you form from that observation?"

"At the time I thought he was being chased."

"Chased? Why was that?"

"Because there was something running along behind the hedge."

"*Behind* the hedge. So not directly threatening him?"

"No."

"And what was it that was running behind the hedge?"

"It was a horse."

"You are certain? – I persist in this question because there has been speculation in some quarters that it may have been human ... a man?"

Harry shook his head. "No, I'm sure it was a horse."

"Didn't you at one time think that it may have been human? I ask you this because of certain reports in the press."

"I only caught a glimpse of it. It was on its hind legs for a moment. That's why I thought it was like a man."

"And there were horses in the field – you have seen them?"

"Yes."

"And a young horse; a foal, if it reared up, could perhaps look like a man?"

Harry agreed. The questions embarrassed him. The running figure had been a mistake that only he and Miranda should have known about, and she should never have said a word to anyone.

Miranda, beautiful in black, had no difficulty with the oath. The coroner, showing that looks held no sway with him, was brisk.

"You told the police at the time that Donovan was being pursued by a man. Is that so?"

She nodded.

"Speak up, we can't hear you."

"I did think it was a man at the time."

"Am I to take it that you have since changed your opinion?"

Miranda's eyes were very wide. "I think so." The coroner riffled his papers impatiently, forcing her to make up her mind. "Yes, I have."

"What brought about this change of opinion?"

"I don't know." Her eyes fell, and she was no more than a confused schoolgirl except, as Harry noticed, the complete black of her clothes outdid the mourning of Donovan's mother.

119

"The opinion you gave at the time gained a considerable degree of publicity ... yet you did not see fit to deny it until recently."

It was unfair. Harry stirred in his seat, but his father put a hand on his arm.

Miranda had bowed her head. "I didn't know anything about the horses in the field when I said it."

"Yet the young man ..." the coroner checked his papers, "Harold Hogge realized almost at once that what was running along the hedge could be nothing but a horse. Why has it taken you so long to reach the same conclusion?"

"I didn't know what was happening." Her eyes were beginning to blur. "I was upset."

"I think it is fair to say that other people were also upset, namely Donovan Brett's family, and this story was not calculated to ease their concern."

"It looked a bit like a man."

"On four legs?"

"He was ... he could have been ... kind of stooped over."

The coroner was unimpressed. "Was it a man?"

Miranda's eyes overbrimmed at last but she made no attempt to brush the tear from her cheek. "It was a baby horse," she whispered, "all longety legs."

Longety legs. She was too childlike. The coroner's expression was frozen. Harry looked into his lap.

120

Neither the firemen who got Donovan Brett down from the tree nor the ambulance crew who carried him away had ever seen a body skewered by a branch, but they had no doubt about what had happened. Brett had climbed and slipped, and had been impaled on a broken, jagged branch that had passed right through his body.

There was nothing to indicate that he had been pursued. A detective sergeant had scoured the ground along the hedge for footprints and had found nothing but the impressions of hooves.

"Which leaves us," the coroner told the jury, "with the question of why this unfortunate young man should have taken it into his head to climb to the top of a high oak tree in the rain. You have heard speculations that he may have been pursued – by man or beast, we know not – but the possibility has been exhaustively investigated and not one scrap of positive evidence has emerged.

"Alternatively, did Donovan Brett, an exceedingly fit young man as you have heard from several witnesses, climb the tree as a test of his strength and daring – which you may think hardly likely in view of the weather prevailing at the time – or is it entirely more plausible that his intention was to play a prank on his friends whose car beneath the tree he must have recognized? It is unlikely that we shall ever know."

The jury agreed that there was nothing sinister in what had happened, and concluded that it was likely to have been a prank. They decided that

Donovan Brett had met his end by misadventure.

The room emptied quietly, the murmur of voices rising only after Donovan's parents had left, alone and silent.

Harry was among the last to leave. His mother sat looking straight ahead, not turning towards him, and would not rise from her seat until all the witnesses had left. Then she rose and, without a word, Harry and his father followed her down the stairs into the entrance hall.

Then she stood immovable and waited until his eyes met hers. "Well," she said, "are you satisfied?"

He made no reply.

"You made those poor people suffer in there with your silly, selfish display. And don't try to play the innocent with me! Not believe in God, indeed! What on earth possessed you to parade your silly opinions on an occasion like this?"

Her indignation had prevented her noticing that the hall had not yet emptied. Harry nodded towards the doorway and, storing her words, she glanced over her shoulder to see that Mr and Mrs Brett had not yet left. They stood near the door talking to someone who at that moment parted from them and raised a hand to acknowledge Harry's parents.

Mrs Hogge drew in her breath. "I think we should leave," she muttered. "One has suffered humiliation enough already." But she was obliged to greet Guy March, who was coming towards them.

He bowed to her but spoke directly to Harry's father. "Sad affair, Hogge. Ghastly for the boy's parents, don't you think?" He looked briefly at Mrs Hogge, raising his eyebrows as if he had asked a genuine question, but as she began to answer he took his eyes from her and addressed Mr Hogge again. "But I'm damned if I can fathom what possessed your son, Hogge. Does he normally behave like that?"

Harry's mother answered. "He caused great distress, I fear, Mr March, and not only to the parents of that poor boy."

"Great distress." March nodded. "He commended himself to no one." He paused until Mrs Hogge was on the verge of replying, then he added, "Commended himself to no one except me."

His eyes, in their chameleon pouches, flickered from Mrs Hogge to Harry's father but did not alight on Harry.

"Unusual boy you have, Hogge. Seems to have the right stuff in him." With the slightest inclination of the head to Harry's mother he turned and left.

CHAPTER THIRTEEN

Harry needed the Duke's Head. He needed Foot's problems as an antidote to his own, and he wanted a drink.

It was easier for him to get a beer at the Duke's Head than at the Pheasant and Trumpet, but it was still not without difficulties, even for Foot himself. Foot's father was the problem. He had once found his son and Harry pulling a pint for themselves when they were well under age and he had chased them out in a terrified frenzy of losing his licence. He was a small, tough man with a quick temper and worried eyes, and the ban on them being seen drinking in his pub had remained even though Mrs Foot, plump and pretty, was much more indulgent.

So, on the day after the inquest, Harry bypassed the forbidden bar and went straight upstairs to the living room of the Duke's Head. Foot's sister was there.

"It didn't take you long to put everything

behind you, Harry," she said, "did it?"

He was puzzled.

"Oh, come on, Harry! One minute you're getting what you want from Miranda, but the minute she's gone you're sniffing round a new one."

"I don't know what you mean."

"I've just been told that Miranda's gone away with her parents to get over it all, is that right?" She did not wait for him to nod. "But don't try to tell me that leaves you on your own because I know different. I've seen you." She turned to Foot. "See, little brother, you boys are all alike." She was as attractive as her mother and had the same high, feminine laugh. "Wonderful, isn't it, the power we women have got over you? And Harry loves it, don't you, Harry?"

Harry always found it easy to talk to Foot's sister. "I quite fancy you, Heather, if that's what you mean."

"And don't I know it. But I'm not offering." She was older than them both by a couple of years, and sometimes helped out behind the bar downstairs. She had experience which they lacked. "Not that I couldn't go for you, Harry. You must have something about you to pull a girl like Miranda."

"Money," said Foot. "He's got the Pheasant and Trumpet."

"Is my brother right?" There was mischief in Heather's face. "Little gold-digger, is she?"

"You're a girl," he said. "You tell me."

"Gives you what you want, does she, Harry?"

She waited for an answer but he simply smiled. "There's always one way to tell." She gazed winsomely at the ceiling and put a hand on her breast. "There's so much for this, so much for that ... and it gets more expensive as it goes down."

"What's your bottom price?" he asked.

Her laughter was shrill. "And I thought I was going to offend you, talking of your girlfriend like that." She slapped at his head, and he cringed away from her to avoid having to answer.

"When you two have finished flirting," said Foot, "I'd like someone to fetch a drink."

"Get it yourself," said Heather. She crossed the room, but at the door she paused and turned. She had not finished with them. "You know what girls are expert in, don't you? And it's not what you think, Harry, and *he*," she nodded at her brother, "doesn't count." She waited for a response from Harry, "Well?"

"If you don't mean sex, I expect you mean love," he said. "Girls are best at love?"

"Maybe they are, but you don't believe it even if you say it. You are a schemer, Harry. It's something you've worked out. Love is a great compliment, so shove it at the girl, dip it in treacle, smear it all over her. You never know, Harry my love, you may just get your hand inside her pants!"

She embarrassed him. It cost him an effort, but he kept his eyes on her and said nothing.

"Got you, Harry! You've gone red. Now you know what I think of you." She had become serious in spite of herself, and she had to go on. "I'll tell you what we are experts in – getting hurt. That's what we know about, Harry Hogge. Getting hurt by the likes of you."

He could see self-pity rising in her even as she struggled to control it, and he looked away, embarrassed for her.

"And you've got me wrong again." She took a deep breath, paused, and when she spoke again her voice no longer trembled. "I'm not thinking of myself, I'm thinking of that girl. And I don't mean Miranda; she can look after herself, that one, even if you do hurt her. As I suppose you will." Her voice became softer, but was tinged with contempt. "There's the other one, Harry – you know who I mean – Emma Judd. I've seen you with her, and it's no use telling me she can look after herself because she's a clever girl, as I suppose she is – but she's also silly. She hardly knows whether she's coming or going, especially with you … with any boy, come to that, so you needn't think you are someone special.

"She's head over heels in love with you … did you know that? Of course you do, or you wouldn't be what you are and she wouldn't be with you every time I see her. So she's going to be hurt. She's lovesick, so when Miranda comes back from her holiday and you go back to her, as you will, that girl Emma is going to be hurt so much my heart bleeds for her."

He remained silent, and Heather smiled at him,

plump and pretty once more. "So now I've told you what's going to happen," she said gaily, "I'm off out." And she left.

Foot spoke to the closed door. "I am strongly of the opinion that my sister fancies you."

"If that's intended to surprise me," said Harry, "it does."

"I surprise myself," said Foot, "quite often. By the way, you promised to do something for me."

"What's that?"

"You said you were going downstairs to fetch a drink."

"I did no such thing."

"Maybe not, but I don't think you are about to refuse. If you do, I shall have to have a word with one or two young women. Which do you prefer?"

"I never bow to blackmail."

"The bitter is good – my father put on a new barrel yesterday."

The old men perched on the bench in the stone corridor, enjoying the discomforts they had grown used to, watched Harry approach with his brass tray.

"Oi-oi," said the first, "what you after, then?"

The old man next to him gave an answer. "Gettin' his hand in early, I reckon."

And the third polished off the routine: "Give him a sniff of the barmaid's apron and he'll be well away."

This triggered them to laugh while Harry stood waiting for a man who blocked the corridor as he talked through the serving hatch to someone behind the bar.

"I'll stay out here, Fred, if it's all the same to you. Don't like to come into the bar in me working clothes," he laughed, "looking like this don't make me all that popular." He had a cheerful face but was encased in black so musky deep he seemed more shadow than substance except that his cheeks glowed as red as coals. "Getting to be like our busy time," he said happily. "Nip in the air this time o' year and they start dropping off the vine. Three funerals today, and another one tomorrow."

He had to lean forward to catch Mr Foot's reply before he straightened, laughing loudly. "You're right, Fred – it's like Christmas trade, good for both of us."

He turned his head. "Sorry, young man, didn't see you there. Customer for you, Fred."

As Harry put the tray on the counter Foot's father winced and immediately put his head through the hatch to see who was in the corridor. "Where's Giles?" he said. "Why didn't he come himself? It'll get me shot if anyone sees me serving you."

"But…" Harry wanted to reason, but Mr Foot was having none of it.

"Never mind your buts – you two will do for me one day!"

This made the undertaker's man more cheerful than ever. "Give the boy a break, Fred. He looks like he could put himself round a pint without too much trouble."

"Pint he will not get. No more than a half for him – if that!" and Mr Foot's head withdrew from the hatch. He yanked open the door behind the bar, pulled Harry inside and ordered him to stand just there, behind the door, where no one in the bar could see him. It was a busy time of day and Mr Foot was called to another customer, leaving Harry neither in the corridor nor out of it.

One of the old men, more talkative than the others and obviously their spokesman, was interested in the undertaker's man. "Did you say you was out three times today?"

"That's right, boss. Crematorium three times, eleven miles each way."

"I know it is; I done it."

"Not in a box, you haven't."

"Not yit."

All the old men laughed, and the undertaker's man with them. "But the travelling isn't all there is to it, not by a long chalk," he said. "There's other things when you get back, which is why I'm still dressed like I'm going to a wedding."

"Some bloody wedding," said the old man, "don't ask me to go wi' you. But you ain't tryin' to tell me your job's all that hard – not like it was when you had to put 'em down a hole. That don't happen much now, do it?"

"You'd be surprised. There's a good many folk go for a proper grave when the time comes."

The old man still had a point to make. "What I mean is there ain't the land, is there, so it stands to reason there ain't going to be so many holes dug. When was the last one you give a proper burial to, for instance?"

"Ah, well now." The undertaker's man thought for a moment. "You remember old Jake Hardcastle, do you? Big feller, tall, held hisself very upright."

"Can't say I do."

"Well, him. He was seccertery to Mr March at Barbican House in the Crescent, which was where he died, funnily enough."

"I don't see nothin' funny in that."

"Well, he didn't live there. He used to have a flat above Todger's shop on the market. You must've seen him. Well, he was the last one I actually physically put underground, as you might say. St Augustine's churchyard, practically next door to Barbican House, that's where he went."

"You didn't have to sweat over that one, then."

"It ain't the travelling so much." The undertaker's man took a drink. "The really hard work is lumping them coffins around when you get there. It'd give you a shock to know what some folks weigh – I'd sooner shift a couple of hundredweight of spuds than some of 'em."

"Bloody sight more use, an' all. I could use you on me allotment."

"But then again, you sometimes get a very pleasant surprise."

"Pleasant?" The old man looked sour. "I shouldn't ha' thought there was much pleasant about your job – it ain't meant to be *pleasant*!"

The undertaker's man was silent, his mind on something else. "He was a big-boned man, Jake Hardcastle – you must have seen him around."

"Still harping on about him, are you? Well, I reckon I do remember him. Always thought he were a schoolmaster; had a kind o' stoop, but he must've been over six foot."

"And heavy with it, would you say?"

"Reckon," the old man agreed. "Do that cost more if he's heavy?" His cronies cackled at that, and nodded when he went on. "You don't bury anyone cheap, that I know for a fact. I figure you must have made quite a bit putting him away, and don't you try to tell us any different."

"Just hold on a bit, boss. All I do is carry the coffin. I don't make anything out of it personally – not as a rule."

"Ah!" The old man had a sharp eye on him. "Not as a rule."

"All right, then." The undertaker's man knew that he had given too much away. "Just to keep you happy … Mr March did give the pallbearers something at that one, but it hardly ever happens and it wasn't what I was talking about, anyway. I was asking how heavy you thought Jake Hardcastle was – fifteen stone?"

"Could ha' bin."

"Fifteen stone at the very least." The undertaker's

man waited until he had been given a grudging nod. "Well, I don't know what he died of, but he must have wasted away something terrible." He gave the three old men time to let that sink in, and then said, "Because when we picked up that coffin in Barbican House it damn near floated to our shoulders it was so light."

"You was thinking of all that beer you was gettin' tret to."

They were still cackling when Mr Foot put the tray into Harry's hand, threw a bar towel over the glasses and sent him away. "And for God's sake don't come back," he said.

CHAPTER FOURTEEN

Sunshine silver-plated the ripples of the river, and when Harry turned his back on it to enter the covered road through the stable block the stored-up greyness of centuries chilled him. At the far end someone was whistling as he washed a car that glinted in the sunlight of the innyard, and when he got closer Harry recognized him. "Baz," he said.

"Harry boy." Their greetings were always curt. The small hard-faced man carried on with his work and Harry was about to walk on when he suddenly noticed it was his car that was being cleaned. He had not seen it since the day Donovan Brett died. "How did that get here?" he asked.

"Police brought it. Yesterday." Baz Boyd wrung out his cloth and began to dry off the windscreen. "It weren't too nice; know what I mean?" He had a narrow, foxy face and his keen eyes rested just long enough to let Harry get his meaning. "Bit of a mess, so I thought I'd get it right for you."

Baz Boyd was the yard man and he knew his rights. Cleaning the car was Harry's responsibility. Harry nodded, thanking him. "You didn't have to do it."

"I know that." Baz looked sidelong at him. "But you wouldn't have liked to ha' done it, know what I mean? Not after what you seen."

"I suppose not." Harry dipped his head. Baz scorned gratitude.

"More than bloody rust, Harry boy. Should've thought the police would've done something their-selves – that's what that young lady say just now when she seen the state it was in." He rubbed hard, whistling between his teeth like a groom. "Went white as cheese, she did, know what I mean?"

"What young lady was that, Baz?"

For answer, Baz nodded towards the shadowy horse stalls and raised his voice. "Ain't that right, Missy? You asked me if there'd been some horri-ble accident."

Harry must have walked past her without seeing her but he knew it was Emma even before she stepped into the open. She seemed alarmed at having been discovered and was too shy to hold his eyes. Neither spoke.

"She say she's lookin' into something from the old days, Harry. I know your dad don't like people pokin' around out here, but I were keepin' an eye on her, don't worry." Baz sniffed without smiling and with great nimbleness emptied his bucket over the cobbles and opened the car door. "If you could just shift your body, Miss, I'll put the motor away." He nodded at several empty stalls that would have been more convenient. "Can't park there, can we, Harry boy? Your guv'nor says them's to be left for the club."

All Harry knew was that his father always wanted the first three stalls kept empty. "What club?"

"That lunch club," said Baz. "Mr What's-his-name and them others. I know it don't meet till tomorrow but you don't want this in the way, do you?" He got into the car.

"Mister who?"

Baz narrowed his eyes and looked swiftly from Harry to Emma and back again. "That's a question, ain't it?" he said.

Emma had seen the look. "I'm sorry, Harry," she said. "I never meant to bother you."

Baz began to back into the space, and Emma was moving away when Harry said, "What did you come here for?" The question was too brusque, and both of them were embarrassed. "I didn't mean it like that."

She nodded. "The car was awful, Harry. I didn't know."

They stood in silence until Baz parked and handed him the keys. "All clean now, Harry boy." He winked at Emma. "Fresh start, if you know what I mean." He walked away leaving her looking at the ground, and Harry unsure what to say. In spite of what Foot's sister had said, they had hardly met since Donovan Brett died.

"I read about it." Emma spoke without meeting his eyes. "It was terrible for you ... and Miranda."

The pause before she added Miranda's name would not have been noticed by anyone else, but it seemed to Harry to shout everything Heather Foot had told him in the upstairs room at the Duke's Head. Could it be that this pale-faced girl with the grey eyes had the kind of feelings for him that he had for Miranda? There was a twisted pleasure in knowing it, a strand of conceit for himself twined with whatever feelings she may have had for him.

"You know what Miranda's parents are like," he said, "they've taken her away for a few days." He tried to smile. "They think she's fragile."

"I was only doing some research, Harry." Emma had to justify herself. "That thing I'm doing about the Mary-Lou ... there seemed to be something at the Pheasant and Trumpet that would help. But it doesn't matter, some other time will do."

"What sort of thing?"

The grey eyes were transparent as they searched his face for any sign that he would find stupidity in what she said. "Maybe it was just one of those old stories, but the Mary-Lou did come from the castle, and it came in and out in some kind of secret way." She frowned. "So I wondered if there really was a secret exit, and I thought of looking here."

"Because we've got cellars?" She nodded, and

he said, "We could go down there and take a look, if you like."

"No," she said quickly. "No." The thought of having to face Mrs Hogge frightened her.

Harry did not press her. He told her of Hobby Hobson's bumps in the night. "I took a look down there myself," he said. "There isn't a sign of an opening anywhere."

"There wouldn't be, because I've looked at the plans of the old town and the Pheasant and Trumpet itself isn't really a suitable place. It's inside where the castle wall used to be."

"So if Hobby Hobson did hear thuds in the night they are coming from some other place."

"They must be."

He felt a twinge of disappointment. "So what were you hoping to find?"

"Well, I have a pretty good idea that there was a gate somewhere near here, and the outer wall of the castle couldn't have been so far away, so I was looking for it." She blushed. "It was pretty silly."

"Baz could have told you where the castle wall was."

"I didn't think to ask him."

The yardman had returned and was placing buckets and mops in the openings of the first three stalls to prevent cars taking the spaces next day. Harry seemed amused. "You can tell her where the castle wall is, can't you, Baz?"

"That I bloody can." He came towards them, directing his words at Emma. "I was all for knocking a bit of it down one day when this young devil here piped up and told me I'd better watch out." He went over to where the stable block opened into the innyard and pointed at a great stone that jutted into the covered road. "That's it – a bit of the castle wall, and but for the boy Harry I'd have knocked it down years ago."

Harry laughed. "I told him a giant put it there, and then we discovered what it really was and found out that nobody was supposed to touch it."

"So it still gets in every bugger's way." Baz went away whistling.

Emma walked into the first of the empty stalls. "I wonder if there's any more of it in here." He went with her, but the side of the stall was built of brick and was plainly of a much later date. But towards the back of the stall there was a door. "Where does this go, Harry?"

It was locked. "It's a staircase to the hayloft up above, that's all." He tried it again but it did not budge. "I always wanted to go up there when I was a kid. There's a room long enough for a cricket pitch, I seem to remember, but the stairs are rotten so it was always too dangerous. That's why this door is kept locked. There's nothing else, just the hayloft."

"Nothing?" He shook his head and she was suddenly so vehement that he was taken by surprise. "I wish there was! I just wish there was a door or a gap or anything where the wall used to be!"

"Why is it so important?"

"If you could see what's happening to my aunt you wouldn't ask such a stupid question! She thinks the only way the Mary-Lou can get out is through her own house. There's got to be another way!"

She was so fierce that he drew back. She saw what she had done and began to apologize but jumbled her words, lost her way and fell silent. She could not face him, and she turned away. He tried to call her back, but she ran.

CHAPTER FIFTEEN

It was no more than a tremble in the air, less even than that, but Harry knew that someone had called him. It was very quiet in his room high above the market place and he put down his book and listened. There was no sound from the corridor outside, but the sensation of hearing his name still echoed in his head and he went to the window and looked down. Cars and people. It was difficult to recognize anyone he knew seen from directly overhead, but a figure hesitated at the kerbside below and then moved swiftly towards the entrance to the Pheasant and Trumpet and was hidden from him by the window ledge.

He turned away from the window and listened again. There was no sound, but the sensation that his name was somewhere being spoken drove him out of the apartment into the corridor. He went downstairs.

"You've been quick," said Anna behind the

reception desk, "I've only just put the phone down. You must have heard it ring."

"Yes," he lied. He looked around the foyer. "Where is she?"

"She's more nervous than ever, Harry. What have you been up to?"

"Nothing." He saw her disbelieving half-smile and acted up to it, even though his heart was thumping. "Well, nothing much."

Anna was satisfied. "The poor girl looked so terrified I couldn't put her in the coffee lounge for people to stare at. She's in the side room." She nodded towards a door in the shadow of the staircase. "Nobody ever goes there, so you'll be quite safe."

Nobody meant his mother. "Thanks, Anna, you're the best."

"Mind you remember it, then." She clucked her tongue and shook her head as he hurried away from her across the foyer. "That boy is going to land himself in trouble."

The side room was used as a cloakroom for a banquet or a ball, and at other times pretended to be an annexe to the coffee lounge although it was only large enough for two tables. Emma sat at one of them.

"I shouldn't be here." She began to get to her feet.

"I knew it was you."

"The girl out there told you."

"I knew it before you reached the door. I was

reading a book and I suddenly heard you say my name ... not on the phone; it was different. You were here and I knew it."

She lowered her eyes and ran her fingertips over the table. He guessed what she was thinking. "It wasn't a voice," he insisted. "I didn't hear a voice. But I knew it was you."

"I've brought a book," she said. It was not a sufficient reason for calling on him, but it was all she had. It was an excuse. What she really wanted was to apologize for having been angry with him the day before, but now he was there in front of her she could not bring herself to say it. "There's something in it I wanted to show you."

There was a briefcase beside her chair and she lifted it to the table and opened it. The book was on top of her papers, all her work. It seemed to embarrass her. "I wish I'd never started," she said. "I think it's driving me insane."

"If you are, so am I." He took the book from her. "I've seen this before, haven't I?"

"I doubt it. There aren't many, and this belongs to the museum. They don't know I have it."

He read the title: *Chadwick's History of Marshland.*

"It's rare," she said, "and I shall have to smuggle it back somehow."

"You've found something important?"

"I don't know. It took a while for me to work it out. Look up Castle in the index."

He did so, squinting, not wanting to put on his

143

glasses, and he had no sooner turned to the page than she took the book from him and sat down. He stood looking over her shoulder. Her shyness seemed to have vanished as she bent over the open page which showed an engraving of the castle ruins as they had appeared to the artist over a century ago. But it was the opposite page, where a plan of the castle was superimposed on a map of the town, that interested her.

"There's not much of the castle left," said Harry. For the most part the diagram consisted of broken lines where long-demolished walls had once stood. More solid was the outline of the remains of the castle keep preserved in the grounds of Barbican House.

Emma put her finger on the page. "Do you see that?" She traced a pair of dotted lines that began at the mound. "That's the tunnel."

"I've been in it," said Harry. "Haven't you?"

She nodded. "When I was small. We went from school, but it hasn't been safe for a long time."

"It never went far, anyway. It's a bit of a disappointment." And even in the diagram the lines petered out before they reached the market place. "That must be where the roof caved in." He sensed that, nevertheless something about the diagram excited her so he tried to live up to her enthusiasm. "But it does seem to be heading in the right direction, towards the Pheasant and Trumpet. There may have been a gate in the castle wall somewhere near."

"I don't know," she said. "It doesn't matter. But look at that." Her finger was near the edge of the page, a long way from the mound. "The moat," she said. "That's the line of the moat, and look at that." Her finger had stopped halfway along the curve of the Crescent. "The houses are built right on top of where the castle wall used to be." Harry nodded; he had always known that. But it was something else that held her attention. "And behind the Crescent there is Moat Lane ... and there, just where my Auntie Rose lives, is that!"

She had bent over the page in her excitement, and he had to lean forward, putting on his glasses to read the small print at her fingertip.

"The sallyport?" he said. "What's that?"

"It's a door in a castle wall where you could sally forth to fight the enemy." Her voice tailed away. She had her elbows on the table and was hugging herself, containing her excitement, but as she looked over her shoulder she found her face very close to his. She was startled, and her eyes opened wide, but he did not move away, and neither did she. She continued to speak. "And the sallyport is a way to get out of the castle and it's right on the edge of the moat."

The last words barely escaped her lips. She allowed her eyelids to droop. Their breath mingled. And then, in the silence that gathered around them, their lips, tantalizing and uncertain, touched. For a moment she was afraid of what she was doing, but the moment drew into seconds and they were still startled by what was happening when the door opened.

Miranda stood there. She saw them. She had entered the room smiling, and the smile remained on her lips. She looked them over, as interested in them as if they were something she had to study, and her smile gradually became aloof. They were beneath her dignity, no longer part of her life; if they ever had been. She took a deep breath, let it out slowly, turned and put them behind her.

Harry followed, needing to speak but in too great a turmoil to know what to say. She reached the centre of the foyer before she stopped and faced him. He opened his mouth but no words formed. He fumbled with his glasses.

"Leave them on," she said, "you look bloody silly either way."

He was left in front of the reception desk. Anna had been watching. "Is there a chance for me now?" she said.

He started to laugh, then thought better of it. Emma was still in the room, and he was about to go to her when he heard a door open at the top of the stairs. He glanced up, and for a fraction of a second even Emma was not in his mind.

Walter Badgett, carrying a tray, had just emerged from the private dining room.

CHAPTER SIXTEEN

Harry stepped closer to the desk. "What's going on, Anna?"

She looked towards the glass doors through which Miranda could still be seen crossing the market. "You should be telling me, Harry." He screwed up his face, not wanting to be questioned. "I can't make out what they see in you," she said. "But that's their business." She was enjoying herself.

"Anna." He gave her time to take her mind off what she had just seen. "Is someone having lunch in the little dining room?"

"You've just seen Walter coming down with a tray. Why ask?"

"But who are they?"

She shrugged. "I wouldn't know that, Harry. It's just something your father arranges."

He paused. It was going to seem a strange question, but he had to ask it. "You've been here all morning, Anna. Did you see any of the club come in and go up the stairs?"

He had made her suspicious. "What mischief are you up to now? I should have thought you'd had enough for one morning."

"Can't you tell me?" he pleaded.

"She's listening, that sweet kid in the room over there. If you are doing anything at all to hurt her after what's just happened, you'll have me on your tail."

"Anna. It's not much to ask."

She thought for a moment. "Well, no, I haven't seen anybody going up to that room, as a matter of fact – but there's been a lot going on, hasn't there, Harry?"

But he was already leading Emma across the foyer and out by the side door.

In the innyard she made him stop. "What have we done?" she said. She turned her head aside when he moved closer. "I never meant any of this to happen!"

"Yes you did." She could not meet his eyes. "Secrets," he said. "I know your secrets. Some of them."

"That's not fair." She spoke to the ground.

"Voices. You hear voices."

She shook her head. "That's all over and done with."

"Not yet." He shook his head. "It's only just starting for me. I heard you this morning when you were nowhere near me. I knew you were saying something. People can do that when they ..." he hesitated, "... when they discover someone they really care about. I heard you."

"It's not the same." But her eyes told him otherwise.

"Hell, Emma," he said, "I want to hear you! I want to know everything about you." He felt able to do anything, and everything was possible. He searched his mind to tell her something to prove it. "I've got a secret. It's not much but it's been bothering me."

He told her about the luncheon club and the secrecy surrounding it. "It's ridiculous, but I want to know. Will you help me?"

"I don't see how I can."

"You've put me on the track already."

They crossed the yard and stood in the mouth of the covered road. "There you are," he said, "all spaces taken." The three stalls that Baz Boyd had kept vacant were now occupied by three cars.

"We knew that yesterday..." She wanted to add his name but was too shy. "It's not a secret."

"But there's no way for them to get to the dining room without going through the foyer – and that they never do. So how?"

He led the way into the end stall and stood by the door in the wall.

"You told me that only went up to the hayloft," she said.

"Yes it does, but the stables are built right up against the back wall of the hotel, so what if there's a way through?"

"Don't you know?"

"I should do." He hunched his shoulders. "There's really nothing up there." A door seemed so unlikely that he did not mention it. "We shall just have to hang about in the yard and see if anyone comes out."

"Hasn't your father got a key?"

"I asked. He says it has been lost for years." He gave the handle a try and turned away.

It was Emma who noticed he had not tried the latch. She lifted it. The door juddered, and jammed at its foot. "I don't think it's locked," she said.

Harry tried again, lifting the door as he pushed. It swung open into gloom and mustiness that seemed to have been undisturbed for generations. But it was as he remembered it. There was a narrow space with a wooden staircase.

He stepped inside. There was so little light that at first he thought it came only through the doorway but, glancing up, he saw that the stairs rose through an opening into an upper floor. Far overhead a grimy window in the roof allowed dim grey light to penetrate.

He began to climb and she went with him. "Close the door," he whispered, "I don't want anyone to follow us."

The thick treads of the stairs creaked and made them keep to the edge where they were firmer, and slowly they came up through the floor into the loft. The room was longer than he remembered it, stretching away into shadows at the far end, beyond the reach of what little light came through the skylights. Harry was about to say something when Emma hushed him.

"Voices," she whispered.

He heard nothing but the hollowness of his own breathing until, softer than the hum of bees, he detected a faint murmur. At first it was difficult to locate but soon they were looking towards the wall nearest to them. It was boarded and whitewashed. "We're very close to the hotel," he said. "We can hear people in the corridors."

The board wall was partly covered by a curtain of old sacking that had been nailed there long ago. They went to it and Harry cautiously pulled the sacking aside, expecting a cloud of dust, but there was nothing but the smell of whitewash and a gap in the boards that had once been a door. But it was a door no longer and there seemed to be nothing but empty space beyond it.

And now he remembered having been forbidden to go beyond the sacking. "It used to be a store room," he whispered.

She hushed him. "Look." She pointed into the darkness beyond the sacking.

Among the shelves lining the walls of the disused store room there was a thread of light. It could only be a door. The voices came from behind it mingled with the sound of dishes being cleared.

"The dining room," Harry breathed. He pictured the little room in his mind. It was years since he had been in it and he could recall no door that could have led into the store room. If there had been a door it must have been covered by furniture. "I didn't know about anything like this."

Emma, believing they had discovered all they needed to know, was about to turn away. He grasped her hand. "Wait. I want to know more."

Dislike of becoming an eavesdropper made her hesitate, but only for a moment. She clasped his hand and became a conspirator. They crept forward and put their heads close to the door.

For a while the clatter of dishes was enough to obscure the voices, but when it ceased someone said, "Thank you, sir. Will that be all?" It was Walter Badgett bowing himself out of the room.

"They've finished." Harry was displeased. "It's all over and we've missed everything."

But someone else was speaking, addressing the whole room. "I am pleased you gentlemen appeared so comatose while Walter was with us – it encourages him to believe we like a little nap after lunch." There was laughter, and the voice resumed. "So we will not be disturbed ... which is particularly important today because I intend to share with you the outcome of my studies."

The speaker paused, but suddenly his voice rang out louder.

"Timekeeper, what is the hour?"

Another voice replied, solemnly picking up a ritual, "The sands run low, Master. The time is at hand."

"Doorman!"

It was a command and a chair was pushed back.

"Doorman, are we secure?"

Footsteps came close and they shrank back and were about to run when the Doorman answered. "I have made the rounds, Master. Our defences are manned."

"Then charge your glasses, gentlemen. I propose a toast."

At this, Harry smiled. He had caught glimpses of many annual dinners in the hotel and seen ceremonials of sashes and aprons. He put his lips close to Emma's ear. "It's all hot air from now on," he said.

"Gentlemen, I ask you to be upstanding and drink to the man whose memory we celebrate, the Constable of the Castle."

"The Constable!"

Chairs were moved as they sat down, and the Timekeeper's voice came again:

"Gentlemen, we have been privileged to visit the Master's home in recent weeks and have seen the result of his diligent researches. We have been the first to know of the discovery of the final resting place of the Constable's servant, about whom so many legends are told. So it is with great pleasure that I now call upon the Master to inform this gathering of the latest stage of his researches."

Harry had his head close to the door, but Emma had ceased to listen. The store room was airless and the mustiness was so heavy that her breath caught in her throat. But there was something else in the air, a sensation that by even listening to what was happening they were being drawn into danger. She tugged at his arm and he was turning towards her when a fresh command rang out.

"Doorman! To your post!"

Almost simultaneously the door handle rattled and someone who was standing so close to the panels that he seemed to shout in their ears cried: "The door is manned!"

"Then call the Wolf!"

They had left it too late. The door had begun to open and they could not run. All they could do was to shuffle to one side as a wedge of light spread across the floor, and they were huddled against the shelves when the man who stood there crossed the store room, hooked up the sacking curtain and stared out into the empty hayloft.

They held their breath, shrinking into the shadows of the shelves. His back was towards them but there was something uncertain about the way the man stood there, as if he was aware he was playing a part in an empty ritual and that the make-believe had gone on too long. But then the voice from within the dining room called him to order.

"Doorman, do your duty!"

The man, gazing into the hayloft, performed his hollow ceremonial. "I am commanded to summon you to our gathering!"

It was a half-hearted attempt at solemnity and he was turning away even before his voice ceased to echo in the long room. They held themselves rigid. Even though they were in deep shadow they would surely be seen.

At the distant end of the room, just beyond the furthest patch of pale daylight, something moved. Emma was aware of it before the Doorman caught a glimpse of it and paused to take a last look at the empty room. There was a heap of old tarpaulins in the far corner. They had been folded and stacked neatly years ago, but part of the stack had collapsed and disentegrated. It was this that had stirred.

Harry heard Emma draw in her breath, then he, too, thinking of rats, saw the rags heave. The Doorman made an exclamation of disgust but could not prevent himself watching. Even when the heap of rags began to crawl towards him he did not move. What he saw had frozen his limbs.

Like a tattered dog the rags came into the first patch of grey light. But there was no sound of paws pattering on the boards. It had no paws. It was not a dog. It was a man, and he was crawling.

At the next patch of light they saw him get off his knees, but he still remained bent with his fingertips touching the floor as if he had difficulty supporting his own weight. He was very thin.

The Doorman held his ground until, with an obscene, swaying rhythm, the tattered, skinny figure increased its pace, scurrying on all fours towards them. It had a bony head blotched with brown, and its jaw hung open. When its teeth, which gleamed white, suddenly chattered, the Doorman could keep his place no longer and stumbled backwards into the dining room unable to take his eyes from what was stalking closer.

The figure was upright now, a man in rags that hung about him like muslin, and his tread was long. Tall, he filled the entrance, and Harry and Emma backed further into the shadows of the room until they were in a corner from which there was no escape.

As the figure advanced, Harry lifted his arm to strike at the repugnant mess, but he was ignored. The figure swept by with a waft of ancient coffin reek that left him blinded and choking. It was Emma who heard the horrified gasp from the men in the dining room before the door slammed shut.

CHAPTER SEVENTEEN

They clattered down the stairs and out into the inn-yard without caring who heard them, and they stood together gasping and waiting for their hearts to cease their painful pounding.

"We've got to get out of here," said Harry. "Somewhere warm." The walls and crooked windows that surrounded them were no longer picturesque and gazed down on them blankly. It was a prison yard.

The questions racing through their minds had no answers. Someone in the dining room had arranged some trickery to terrify the others, but why? It had to be a masquerade, a fake, but why the graveyard reek that came with it?

"One thing is certain," said Harry, "I'm not keeping watch out here to see who leaves that place."

"The one who came out of the dining room to call it," said Emma, "the one they called the

Doorman … I thought I recognized him." Harry raised his eyebrows, asking the question, but she shook her head. "I'm not sure." She was trembling. "I think I ought to go home, Harry."

"Not yet." He had some vague idea of them both confronting his father and telling him what they had seen. He hinted at it, then added, "He wouldn't like it, though; he'd say I'd been spying."

"I know."

They went into the hotel through the side door with his mind still on his father, wondering if he would be in the office.

"I hope not," said Emma. "I don't want to see anyone."

He stopped abruptly. "Did I speak just now?" he asked.

"You were wondering if your father was in his office."

"But I didn't say so … not aloud."

She was about to contradict him when she fell silent. No, she had not heard him. His voice had not come from outside. She had known what was in his mind without him saying anything. They paused at the corner of Anna's desk, each trying to fathom what was happening when a noise from across the foyer interrupted them.

"I don't give a damn what he thinks!" The voice from the staircase was loud. "This time he's gone a bloody sight too far!"

The man was on the first landing. His face was flushed, and he was bending stiffly from the waist

158

to make his anger carry towards the alcove of the private dining room.

"Tell him that I quit his bloody rotten little club and he'll see no more of me!"

From where they stood they could not see the door of the dining room but it was obvious that it stood open, for they could make out that someone more in control of himself was remonstrating with the man.

"No, I will not go out through the back way! Nothing will induce me to go that way ever again. Nothing!"

His last word was a shout, and with it Harry heard the door of his father's office open.

Mr Hogge did not allow himself to be ruffled. He came into the foyer pulling at the cuffs of his jacket and smiling as if he was about to greet a new guest. He put one foot on the bottom stair and, looking up, spoke to the man's back. "Good afternoon, sir. Is there anything I can do for you?"

Harry had seen his father deal with awkward clients before, and it was always a pleasure to watch. He never raised his voice and nothing disturbed the calm smile or the look of sad concern on his face. The man had not heard him.

"Sir, can I help you?" Mr Hogge repeated.

"Yes, you damn well can!"

The man spun around and Mr Hogge's smile vanished. "What are you doing there?" he asked. "I thought you were still in session."

"And so we damn well are!" The man turned his

back on the dining room. In the shadows of the hayloft they had not seen his face, but it was the Doorman. They were certain. Emma hid herself behind Harry as the man came down the stairs. "And they can stay in session as long as they like because I shall never join them again – never!"

Harry's father glanced around the foyer just as a couple came into the hotel and went up to the reception desk. He kept his voice low. "We can certainly sort this out," he said. "Let's have a word about it in my office."

"Damn your office!" The man, red-faced and heavily built, was going to charge through all niceties. "They've just pulled a trick on me I find so offensive that I've told them what they can do with their club and their mumbo-jumbo. Do you know what I've just seen wandering in through that back door they have up there?" He waved his hand above his head to dismiss everything behind him, and gave Mr Hogge the chance to pacify him.

"Maybe they do overdo it a bit," he said, but he only triggered more anger.

"Overdo it! How would you like a shambling great stinking skeleton coming at you out of the dark in that place you've got above those stables! That was no joke, Hogge."

Harry's father smiled at the couple at the desk. "Look after these people would you, Anna, and I'll be with you in a moment."

As a distraction it was not completely success-ful. "They'd rigged up something horrible up there, Hogge. You'll have to do something about it or the reputation of this place will go downhill hell for leather – and I personally can vouch for that!"

"Of course." Mr Hogge was at last able to shepherd him towards the office. "I shall certainly see that something is done."

Indignation was being replaced by grumbling. "When I joined them they were just a little group of friends with an interest in history, and all the mystery stuff was just a little bit extra, but now..." The office door closed.

"So now we know," said Harry.

"I don't want to talk about it."

The market place was too noisy for them to talk properly in any case, and even when they reached the side streets they were still dumb. Harry glanced at the girl alongside him.

"I'm not Miranda," she said, not looking at him.

He was barely startled. "You're reading my mind again."

"No." She shook her head. "You were looking at me, so it would be very strange if you weren't comparing me with Miranda. I was doing it myself." The grey eyes were steady on him. "I like her."

"Everyone does."

"Especially you."

"Does that worry you?"

"Yes," said Emma. "She's still lovely, no matter what's happened."

He nodded, his eyes fixed on hers. "It's the shape of the face I like," he said, "quite small, and she has a nice blunt little nose, and black hair …" Emma dipped her head shyly but he did not stop "… and eyes that frighten you to death. Grey, and they want to know too much."

The eyes ceased to look at him, but he continued to speak, and they continued to walk, but they chose all the quietest places and stopped from time to time.

They lingered in Moat Lane, and when they came to the little square she once more hid behind him, but it was useless. Aunt Rose's door opened.

"You wasn't going to walk right past without coming to see me, was you?" She shook her stick at them, and Harry went forward but she told him, "I wasn't talking to you – not yet." She tilted her head as though to speak around him. "You ain't ashamed of your old auntie, are you?"

Emma came out from behind him but her excuses were cut short.

"Fetch him indoors." Aunt Rose turned her back on them and they were obliged to follow her inside. Harry did not move carefully enough around the hatstand so that he brushed a picture with his shoulder and made it crooked, and in the dimness he stumbled over a step and half fell into the crowded living room. He had to steady himself against a table.

"He ain't been drinkin', have he?"

"No," said Emma.

"Because if he have, there's no tellin' what damage he might do." She sat in her chair, both hands on top of her stick and frowned on him as she continued to speak to her niece.

"Where do he come from?"

Emma told her.

"Hotel? Then he can get his hands on drink any time, day or night."

"I'm sober," Harry protested.

"I ain't goin' to say a word about it," said Emma's aunt. "If you can't hold yourself upright you'd better sit your bum down, Harry Hogge."

Emma was anxious and began to say that they would soon have to be on their way, but she was ignored.

"Me legs is me downfall." Crossing the tiny room leaning heavily on her stick had made Aunt Rose out of breath. "Have you got half-decent legs, Harry Hogge? Because if you have, you want to take care of 'em – treat 'em right and they won't run amock." Having decided to speak to Harry, she nodded her head towards Emma. "What d'you think of this little old girl, then?"

"Well…" Harry was embarrassed.

"You don't sound any too sure o' yourself."

Emma broke in. "We've really got to go."

"Oh my God!" Her aunt suddenly started up in her chair and pressed a pudgy hand to her bosom. "I ain't ever had such a fright in the whole o' my born days, and that's the truth."

"What's wrong, Auntie?" But Emma was

163

waved back and told to sit down.

"If I was to breathe one word of what happened to me not twenty-four hours gone by, I'm sure I'd drop dead as a cinder in that there grate. Would you stir up the fire for me, my Sugar?"

Emma stooped to the fire and rattled the ash from beneath the coals. It was warm in the little room, and the heavy curtains made it dim. She watched Harry as he found a low armchair with an ornate wooden back and sat stiffly upright.

"He don't say a lot, that young feller in the corner over there. Is he always like that?"

"I do speak sometimes," said Harry.

"You ain't like me, then. Emma will tell you, I hardly ever have a word to say to no one – which is just as well, because what I could say would set the blood cursing through your veins wi' fear. But that little old girl over there, bless her heart, will have to tell you what it is because I ain't saying a single solitary word. Me lips is sealed." Her eyes were fierce in her plump face and her lips were screwed as tight as the knotted end of a balloon.

"He knows about the voices, Auntie," said Emma.

"And the horrible murder?"

Emma glanced quickly at Harry. "He thinks … we both think that Mr Pascoe getting murdered just after we heard the voices must have been a coincidence."

"That ain't what I was talkin' about at all, you silly girl! I mean the dreadful murder of that poor

164

young man stuck up the tree. That was the Mary-Lou done that, and don't you try to tell me different." Her angry gaze was fixed on Harry. "That's what the Mary-Lou always done to them. Skewered them up somewhere like a butcher, so as he could come back and get at them when he wanted a bite o' fresh meat!"

There was silence. She looked from one to the other. "That ain't something you want to know about, is it? That ain't too dainty, I know, but that's the truth – and I tell you somethin' else you maybe don't want to know, but I'm the one inflicted with it and there ain't nothin' I can do to help it."

The thought of what had happened to her made her indignant and she glared at Harry as if he was responsible. "Well, let me tell you this, and then I shall be silent for evermore." She pointed across the room. "What do you think that ironing board is propped up in that corner for? Have you ever seen me welcome guests to my sittin' room with ironing boards clutterin' up the place so as you can hardly move for 'em? No, you never have, but there it is right at this very moment, and I'll tell you for why."

She paused, looked from one to the other, and then exclaimed, "Because I had to shift it from that there cupboard!" She lifted her stick and banged at the door of the cupboard next to the fireplace. It swung open. "There now, that's empty, ain't it? That's empty because that ironing board has taken to jumpin' and bangin' about in the night so much that I was frit half out of me skin. And I've heard a rumblin' and a bumpin' as if something was trying to come through."

She paused, and looked carefully at Harry, judging his reaction. "And a voice," she said. "I heard a voice, and you needn't mock this time, young feller, because it were a real voice ... far, far away and not one of them other kinds of sounds which your sort pours scorn on."

"No," said Harry, "not me." He wanted to be as much a part of what was happening in the dim, warm room as Emma. "There are things going on which I'd never guessed."

"Ah." Aunt Rose let out her breath in a long sigh. Her face was full of smug knowledge. "And things going on which you never will know, because I ain't going to tell you."

"Why not?" He had caught her off guard. "Emma would like to know."

"You keep Emma out o' this!" Her reaction surprised them both. "I don't want no pretty little old girl like her mixed up with coffins and corpses ..." she drew in her breath, "and far worse things than that!" She jabbed her stick at the open cupboard. "There's a man dead somewheres about – and there's going to be another one before long. I heard 'em talking about it, I heard 'em!"

Emma got to her feet and went to her aunt. Only the table separated them from Harry but he could not hear what they murmured with their heads close together. After a few moments Aunt Rose took a handkerchief from the pocket of her dress and wiped her eyes while Emma gently shut the cupboard door and dropped the latch. Aunt Rose had no more to say.

CHAPTER EIGHTEEN

"Were you asking for my son?"

Emma turned from the reception desk, where she had been speaking to Anna, to find herself facing Harry's mother. For a moment she was too nervous to reply and Anna came to her rescue. "I've rung the apartment, Mrs Hogge, but can't get a reply."

Harry's mother ignored her and spoke directly to Emma. "Does he expect you?"

"I don't know."

"I haven't seen you here before," said Mrs Hogge. "Do I know you?"

Anna broke in. "I'm so sorry, Mrs Hogge. I should have introduced you – this is Emma Judd." Her smile took in both of them but only Emma responded.

"I doubt if it's worth your while waiting." Mrs Hogge looked over her head. "He has probably gone out by now to meet his young lady."

She was mistaken. Harry was on his way downstairs but had been delayed on the first landing. He had heard the phone ring but had ignored it, certain it was Emma. "Good morning, Mrs Burton," he said to a woman pushing a cleaner's trolley.

"You look as if you've got something to be cheerful about, young Harry."

"Do I?"

"Cat's been at the cream." Mrs Burton was no one's idea of a chambermaid. She refused to wear hotel uniform and was often taken for a guest. She was not a favourite of Harry's mother. "You're the lucky one."

"Lucky?" said Harry. "Me?"

"So who is she?"

He kept his face blank.

"The girl downstairs," said Mrs Burton. "She's second string to your bow, I suppose – in case Miranda gets snaffled up by someone else."

He would have told her how wrong she was, but his mother was coming up the stairs. "I see you are out of bed at last, Harold." It was his in-front-of-the-staff name.

"Saturday morning, Mother, and I did get in a bit late last night." He had been with Emma until the last bus to her village. Neither of them had wanted to use his car.

"You were more than just a bit late, Harold. I heard you come in."

"I hope I didn't wake you."

"I never sleep until I know you are indoors." His

mother drew in her breath as she considered whether to continue to speak in front of Mrs Burton, who was always liable to join in uninvited, but she could not resist the chance to chastise him. "And if you kept Miranda out until all hours, I'm ashamed of you."

"He's a lucky lad," said Mrs Burton. "She's a lovely girl, that one."

Mrs Hogge was irritated but had to agree. "A very nice girl. And her parents have *standards*, Harold, I want you to remember that."

"These young chaps don't always do what you want them to, do they, Mrs Hogge?" Mrs Burton looked at Harry and then back to his mother. "But I expect he'll get round you in the end, like they always do."

"Thank you, Mrs Burton." Harry's mother had had enough. "There are beds to be made and a room to be cleaned." She unlocked a door and allowed Mrs Burton to push her trolley through before she turned around and said, "By the way, Harold, there's some girl downstairs who wants to see you. I can't imagine who she is."

"She's the one I was with last night," he said.

Mrs Burton paused in the doorway. "Who's been a naughty boy, then?"

"Kindly get on with your work, Mrs Burton!"

Mrs Burton winked at Harry and obeyed.

"So you were not with Miranda last night." His mother was glacial.

"No. Not Miranda."

"So who is this girl downstairs … this Emma Judd?"

"Just a girl I know."

"*Just* a girl – then why is she calling here to see you? I hope you are not telling me you prefer a girl like that to Miranda!"

"A girl like what?"

"A girl who…" Mrs Hogge was rarely flustered, but she saw from Harry's face that she had blundered. "You know very well what I mean! There was something too bold about her, far too bold."

"Too bold? Emma?"

"She may try to look like a timid little thing, but when she turned those eyes on me I didn't know where to look. It was as if she saw right through me."

"She does that to me, too," said Harry. He smiled at his mother, and she searched his face for several seconds before she turned away to give Mrs Burton a bad time.

When Harry got down to the foyer it was empty. "She wouldn't wait in here," Anna told him. "She's outside."

"My mother?"

Anna nodded, and Harry was on his way out and in no mood to turn back when his name was called. He paid no attention, but it happened again and he turned to see his father beckoning. He had Guy March at his side and seemed peevish. "Mr March wants a word with you," he said.

The puffy eyes scrutinized Harry, but when

March spoke it was to Harry's father. "We know the young man has the courage to speak his mind, Hogge; the incident at the inquest told us that." He watched Mr Hogge's reaction, and chuckled when he saw it. "But in spite of what you think, I admire the boy, Hogge. The question is – can he keep his own counsel?"

Harry's father looked to his son to answer for himself.

"I should think so." Harry was cautious. "It depends on what it is, I suppose."

March, detecting defiance in Harry's response, spoke to his father with the air of putting Harry to the test. "You tell me he witnessed the outburst on the stairs the other day. What else does he know?"

"Only what he saw. Isn't that so, Harry?"

The incident was a difficulty between them. Harry had tried to speak to his father about it, even wanting to confess that he had eavesdropped on the luncheon club, but his father had brusquely dismissed the whole matter.

"There was a bit of a row on the stairs about something," Harry said, "but I couldn't make it out."

"It was just a bit of tomfoolery among some old friends that went wrong," said his father, turning to March to confirm it.

"Very well put, Hogge. Spoken with the tact of a true hotelier. Take a lesson from him, young man." March was in high good humour. "But, heavens above, that was certainly an angry man on the stairs the other day!" He shook his head, then suddenly and sharply directed all his attention on Harry. "You are alone at this moment? No one with you, waiting for you?"

"No." The lie came out so pat that it surprised Harry himself, and he gazed closely into the pouches to see if the eyes lurking there believed him. Apparently they did.

"Because I would like you to run a small errand for me, and it is important that it should be performed with tact." March smiled. "With great discretion, if you follow me?"

Harry's curiosity was aroused. "I won't say anything about it, if that's what you mean."

He watched as March reached into an inner pocket and drew out a small, flat packet. "It is just a little gift," he said, "to let that very angry friend of ours realize that none of us bears him any ill will. Look, I will show you," and he opened the packet and took out a leather wallet. "I would send it by post, but it is rather important that he should get it as soon as possible to prevent ill temper rankling in his bosom, you understand?"

He spoke lightly, and Harry held out his hand to take the package, but March held it a moment longer.

"I would take it myself, but perhaps it is too soon after the event. Look, it contains a note which I am very concerned should be put in his hand without delay. I need a trustworthy person." He had opened the wallet so that Harry should see the envelope, and now he sealed the package and glanced at Harry's father. "One can't be too careful, Hogge. Does your boy know how much our little group values the way you protect our anonymity?"

"Harry and I have never even spoken of it." He turned to his son. "It's a private luncheon club, Harry. They like to keep themselves to themselves."

"I understand." Harry nodded, avoiding his father's eye. "That's the first I've heard of it, Mr March."

"Good." Almost reluctantly March placed the package in Harry's hand. "Very good. I believe I have chosen the right man for the task." He released the package. "Excellent. Into his very hand, dear boy, and mum's the word." A nervous gleam had appeared on his pitted skin. "You shall be rewarded."

Harry shook his head. "I shall be glad to do it for you, Mr March."

Outside, he found Emma. "Let's get away from here, quick," he said, "I'm not supposed to be with you." She stood stock still, and it took him a long moment to realize what he had said. "No, it's not that." He reached for her hand but she shrugged him away. "It's nothing to do with my mother."

"She doesn't like me, Harry."

"She doesn't know you – and she doesn't know half of what we know. Nobody does." He had something to tell her but it was more urgent to move away from the hotel. She went with him.

"I've just been let into secrets," he said. "I've met the Master of the luncheon club." He paused, glancing back at the Pheasant and Trumpet. The glass door swung and Guy March came out. "That's him," he said, "and I've just been talking to him. I recognized his voice." He hurried her around a corner. "He didn't see us, did he?"

She also glanced back. "Why is it so important?"

"Because I told him I had no one with me. And I also know exactly who the Doorman is because I'm taking a message to him right now." He was showing her the package when he exclaimed, "Dammit! I don't know where to take it – it was all so secretive he forgot to tell me where the Doorman lives!"

Emma spoke quietly. "But *I* know," she said.

CHAPTER NINETEEN

"The Doorman," said Emma, "is Mr Eggleton. I recognized him on the stairs. I know where he lives."

"Why didn't you tell me you knew him?"

"I didn't want anything more to do with it. I was afraid, Harry. It wasn't just that horrible thing in the hayloft, whatever it was."

"They were playing games ... it was someone dressed up."

"Well, it frightened us both at the time, and when I saw Mr Eggleton on the stairs in such a bad temper and realized he was one of them it made me feel even worse."

"So you knew the Doorman all the time," said Harry.

"And I've even been to his house. He has records of all sorts of things in there, Harry – he couldn't have been more helpful when I was writing all that stuff about the town. He knows so much about names and families that I couldn't have done it without him. He's a nice man, and he likes to talk."

Harry thought of the day the papers were blown from her hand as she stood on the bridge. "I'm glad you wrote that history," he said, "and I'm even more glad it blew away and I picked it up."

He had the urge to put everything else aside to tell her how unusual she was, but her determination was not to be deflected. "That's as may be, Harry Hogge, but it's got nothing to do with where we're going now."

"When I've delivered this," he tapped the pocket containing the package, "all that horrible stuff is over and done with."

"You sound sorry."

"Maybe. Don't you feel there's still a bit of a mystery about it all? Something we don't know?"

"And don't want to know."

"If you really felt like that about it you wouldn't be so keen on coming with me to see the Doorman."

"Ex-Doorman. You'd get lost without me."

They were in a tree-lined avenue where the hedges were tall and the houses were large. She wanted to wait at James Eggleton's gate. "Nobody's supposed to know about this except you, Harry," she said. "I don't want to get you into trouble with Mr March."

But she had no choice. Harry walked up to the front door alone, but as Mr Eggleton took the package his attention was caught by something beyond Harry. "Who's that lurking at the end of the drive?" he said. "Don't I know her?" And he immediately stepped forward and beckoned. "That must be Emma. Come forward, Emma Judd."

The face that had been flushed and angry when Harry had first seen it was now smiling and benign. Eggleton shook Emma's hand. "Where has my favourite student been all this time? Come in and tell me how your great work is progressing." He was so concerned with Emma that he almost shut the door on Harry. "I'm sorry, young fellow." He pulled his glasses down his nose and looked over them. "You seem strangely familiar. Where can I have seen you?"

When Harry mentioned the Pheasant and Trumpet, James Eggleton's face became solemn. "Oh," he said. "Oh dear. Well, never mind," and he immediately turned away to speak to Emma. "You promised to show me your work," he chided her. "Bad girl – you were doing so well."

"I lost some pages." She told him about the bridge and the gale. "Harry saved some of it."

"Good man. Top marks." He led them into a room stacked and littered with books. "But no harm done; it can all be rewritten."

"But I'm afraid I lost some notes as well as my manuscript," Emma admitted, "and I can't remember it all."

"Wicked, wicked girl. And I suppose you were

too shy to come to see me and confess it. Couldn't face the dragon, is that it?" He chuckled. "So at what point does your story peter out?"

"The Constable of the Castle." Emma seemed to have forgotten their reason for being with him. "I couldn't remember all the details of what he did to keep the people in order." She reddened, realizing the connection between the Constable and what she and Harry had overheard being said in the private dining room. She had forgotten she was in the Doorman's presence. "But it doesn't matter," she tailed off.

"Connections, connections." Eggleton ran a hand over his bald head. "You must remember, Emma, that everything is connected to everything else, and names are the strongest links of all. Take the most obvious – there is a direct line from Gilles du Marais, the very first Constable, to the present incumbent of what remains of the Castle. *Marais*, as I must have pointed out to you, means *marsh* in French, and it is only a small step from that to *march*. There is an unbroken line, I think you'll find, between Gilles du Marais and Guy March." He sighed and gazed at his bookshelves. "And as with names, so with character – the line continues."

He fell silent, lost in a train of thought, and they waited. He came to himself with a start. "Where was I? Far away. Lost in antiquity. Disregard what I have just said – far too fanciful. Mr Guy March would never indulge in the necromantic practices of his forebears." He smiled wryly. "Or not in any way that you'd notice. He's a nice enough fellow, is Guy, a good friend of mine, and he'd never indulge in the casting of spells like his ghastly ancestor."

He fixed his eye on Harry. "And what say you, young man of the Pheasant and Trumpet Hotel, are you interested in names and the casting of spells?" He once more looked over his spectacles. "Except, of course, for the spell that Miss Emma Judd casts; that is a different matter entirely."

Harry had seen Emma lower her head bashfully, so he changed the subject. "I only brought the message," he said.

"What message?"

"You have it in your hand."

"Have I? Good heavens, so I have." Eggleton looked at the package as if seeing it for the first time. "What an absent-minded old fool I'm becoming. Now let me see." He picked up a paper knife from a pile of letters on the floor and slit the package open. "A wallet? How strange. And a note tucked into it. Who sent me this, young man? And why?" But before Harry could answer he had opened the envelope and taken out a sheet of paper. He read it in silence, and when he had finished he raised his head and clucked his tongue. "And when Mr March gave you this," he asked Harry, "how did he seem? What was his manner?"

"He said it was an apology." Harry was reluctant to remind James Eggleton of his outburst on the stairs, so he added, "I'm not sure what it was about."

"No, of course not." Eggleton was replacing the envelope in the wallet when he paused. "Ah, and there's something else, just as he says." He shook what appeared to be a scrap of grey material, a piece of cloth, on to his palm, but immediately drew back his head with an exclamation of disgust. "It reeks!" he said, and even across the room they detected the stench of rot.

Holding the scrap at arm's length he went to the fireplace and threw it on the flames. "My friend has a strange sense of humour and is too fanciful by half," he said. "He calls it a message from the past." He rubbed his palm vigorously as he showed them out. "It's a message I'd rather not have received." He laughed ruefully. "And there is no reply."

CHAPTER TWENTY

"She wants to see you," said Emma.

"Can't think why," said Harry. "She doesn't think much of me."

Emma spoke shyly. "She says someone your size must have some use in him."

Aunt Rose sat as usual in her chair, ready to pass judgement.

"Have you cut down on your drinkin' yet, Harry Hogge?"

"Well…" he began and looked towards Emma for a clue as to what he should say but she, embarrassed, had lowered her eyes.

The stick rapped the floor. "And you don't have to look over there for your answer, young feller. Have you, or have you not, given up the drink?"

Emma's eyelids lifted and her grey eyes looked sidelong at him. He had never seen a face so pretty and so secretive.

"What do I want with drink?" he said, and he

saw the eyelids lowered again.

Aunt Rose had missed nothing. "I seen some temptations in my time," she said, "but I never seen anything like what's goin' on between you two. Never! So you better take care or there'll be trouble."

"Auntie," said Emma, "you don't have to bother about us."

"But that's just what I do have to do!" She snatched suddenly at Emma's hand. "This girl have got to have someone who's right for her, and she have got her heart set on you, Harry Hogge!"

Emma's face was flushed. "Don't say things like that, Auntie."

"I've got to, my Sugar. These young men always lets a girl down."

"Not me." Both faces turned towards Harry, but he spoke only to Emma. "Not me," he repeated. "Not ever."

It was the oath he had not given at the inquest. It brought silence to the little room and caused him to look at his feet.

Aunt Rose released her niece's hand. "You're a great clumsy lummox, Harry Hogge, but maybe you can make yourself useful."

She reached with her stick and tapped the cupboard beside the fireplace. "Open that door and take a look inside. No, not you," she said as Emma moved forward, "this is a job for a man."

"Have you been hearing things again?" Emma asked, but her aunt frowned and silenced her.

Harry opened the door. There was nothing in the cupboard except the ironing board that had been propped up in the living room last time he was there. "I ain't got no other space for it," said Aunt Rose. "Take it out."

He did so.

"Now what do you see?"

"It's empty."

"Empty!" she echoed. "But that slitherin' and scratchin' I told you about goes on and on, night after night. Have I got rats, Harry Hogge? Do you see any rat holes?"

Harry examined the cupboard with care. At some time, long ago to judge by the pattern, the walls of the cupboard had been papered over. He ran his fingers over the trelliswork design of blue and pink flowers but the walls were smooth and there were no cracks. He tapped, but the brickwork behind the paper was solid. The floor was covered with a square of linoleum so old that its pattern had worn away. He rapped it with his knuckles; it was lumpy but firm.

"There aren't any rats," he said.

He glanced over his shoulder and saw a look of triumph on Aunt Rose's face. "I know there ain't no rats," she said. "It's somethin' bigger nor rats. Do you lift that lino, Harry Hogge, and tell me what you see."

It took him some time, and Emma had to find him an old kitchen knife before he was able to raise a corner of the lino and peel it back. The years had welded it to the brick floor, but as he tugged at it something else became visible. In the centre of the cupboard floor there was a circular iron manhole cover.

Aunt Rose was standing over him, leaning on her stick. "That's it!" she exclaimed. "Told you it was there!"

She had told him nothing of the sort, but she had already turned to speak to Emma. "I was layin' in my bed last night puzzling my mind about what was goin' on, and thinkin' and thinkin' about this old house and what my daddy used to tell me when I were a little tiny girl, and suddenly I thunk what he used to tell me. He used to say: 'You got to keep away from that particular spot, girlie, or else you'll get yourself drownded.' That's what he say, and I must've been only a little mite because I was only six years old when he died, and ain't it a funny thing but I hardly remember him goin' yet I do remember him sayin' to keep away from that there old cistern."

She rapped it with her stick. "And there it is! That haven't been of any use since this old house got tap water, and that was donkey's years ago, and then my father must've covered it up so's I couldn't get at it." She laughed. "We've had a fair bit o' rain recently, haven't we?"

She looked at both of them, and when they agreed it had rained quite heavily, she said, "Then it's just been that rainwater runnin' and tricklin' into that old tank that's started my poor old mind runnin' away downhill as fast as you like, and no stoppin' it."

"And running water does sound like voices, Auntie," said Emma. "It babbles away to itself."

"I'm that relieved, I can't tell you! To think of me laying in bed and worrying meself silly with all them old tales of the Mary-Lou and wonderin' how someone could have baited me to make it come after me."

Harry stood up. "Baited you?" he asked.

Aunt Rose sat down heavily. She was out of breath, and she waved a hand to allow Emma to tell him.

"It's horrible," said Emma. "It's something the Constable used to do to anyone he wanted to do away with. He'd pretend to be pleased with them but somehow or other he'd bait them so that, when they had left him, the Mary-Lou could track them down and kill them."

"That's what he done." Aunt Rose nodded. "And there was me layin' abed upstairs and thinkin' I'd been baited. It don't bear thinkin' of." Suddenly she leant forward. "What do you think you're doing now, Harry Hogge?"

He had straddled the cistern cover and had bent to grasp the iron ring in its centre. "Just making sure it's not overflowing," he told her.

She was pleased. "He ain't such a bad old boy," she said to Emma. "That old lid's too heavy for you or me."

"Maybe for me as well." Harry was having

difficulty, but suddenly it freed itself and he lifted it easily. "It's black down there. I can't see a thing."

"I keep a torch by my bed. Go you upstairs and fetch it, Emma."

When she had gone, Aunt Rose said, "Harry Hogge, do you really care as much as you say for that little girl o' mine?"

He looked at her steadily, but said nothing. She examined him, her sharp eyes probing into his, but he did not flinch, and after a while she turned away. "Well, that's all right then," she said, and was immediately sharp with Emma. "So, give him the torch, girl, and let him get on with it!"

The beam was too weak to show the surface of the water. "At least it's not going to overflow," said Harry, "it's nowhere near full."

He dropped a fragment of lino into the blackness but forgot to listen for it hitting the water. He was distracted by what he saw. His beam had picked out the sides of the shaft. It was of stone, roughly cut, and projections that could have been steps jutted from the wall except that they ceased long before they reached the bottom.

And there was something else that made him slide the lid back into place and stamp it down. From somewhere below a draught of air had gushed upwards into his face. It brought with it a reek of foulness that made him snort and draw back. It was the same reaction that the Doorman had made in his book-lined room, and the smell from the fragment of rag in the wallet was identical.

CHAPTER
TWENTY-ONE

Guy March was full of regret as he approached the
gate to the tunnel. He had put himself in danger.
Events were overtaking him, and he had only
himself to blame. Night had fallen, and it was welcome, but was it dark enough? – would it ever be
dark enough to protect him?

He threw back his head and gazed up at the
stars. Why had he been such a triumphant brag-
gart as to summon the Mary-Lou to his presence
in the Pheasant and Trumpet? It was that which
had made Eggleton desert him in such a rage that
he had become a danger that now had to be dealt
with. And, no matter what happened tonight, the
risk of being discovered would not end.

March unlocked the gate, but paused before he
pushed it open.

Within the house the card-player detected his
reluctance. "You are unhappy, my love?"

"A little troubled," he admitted.

He was aware of the irritated flutter of the cards and knew he could not deceive her. "It is the question of opening this gate and letting our servant loose," he said.

"He has a task to perform this night. It must be done!"

"Yes, yes." He spoke hastily. "It is not the task – it is this gateway that is the problem. It is his only exit, and from here he must cross the lawn and climb the wall. Some night he will be seen … and then there will be questions. We shall be invaded."

"Let him loose!"

"If there were only another way…" His words were cut short by a thud that came rumbling to him from the tunnel's throat.

She, too, had heard it, and her words were whips that drove him underground.

His light trembled against the walls as if it was the tunnel itself that threatened to collapse on him but he felt his way forward, deeper and deeper underground, until the coffin stood before him. Something was amiss. His heart missed a beat. The lid, which he had replaced with a pulley and grapples, lay crookedly. And the coffin was empty.

He turned, shining his light back along the tunnel. "I must have passed him along the way." His voice was small and full of fear, but a second thud and a sudden scrabbling on the stonework made him spin around to face the coffin once more.

The sound crawled closer. It came from the

cavity in the wall from which he had levered the coffin, and a moment later the skeleton of a hand and arm appeared and gradually, like a parasite emerging from some creature it had sucked dry from inside, the Mary-Lou emerged.

In that moment Guy March knew his troubles were over. The Mary-Lou would never need to use the gate again. The coffin itself should have told him so. It had been used to seal the opening and mark the entrance to the hidden path that the Mary-Lou had used when it sallied forth to obey its first master long ago. Time had allowed rubble to choke the gap. But now, the better to serve its new master, the Mary-Lou had cleared its secret passage to the outer world.

CHAPTER TWENTY-TWO

It was getting late, and two people who were not yet asleep had reason to be thinking of Emma and Harry.

Aunt Rose left things as they were and went to bed. That boy Harry Hogge had set her mind at rest, and it was somehow a comfort that he had helped her rediscover the old cistern that Dad made such a fuss about, all them years ago. But he were like that, my old Dad, and there ain't no danger of me falling down that hole any more, the size I am now.

She chuckled to herself as she eased her bulk up the stairs one at a time, resting at each one and going through it all again in her mind. There ain't no point in putting back that ironing board and all them other things until I've found a new bit of lino for that floor. But that can wait and oh, that bed do look cosy.

It took time to get undressed and into her

night-gown, and then to heave herself into the most comfortable position and settle down. It was a blessing that she was so tired because she would soon be asleep.

Before many minutes had passed Aunt Rose was breathing gently and did not hear metal slide on stone within the cupboard downstairs, nor hear the latch raised as the cupboard door swung open in her dark parlour.

James Eggleton kept late hours. Those young people were on his mind. She was a clever girl, no doubt about that, and that boy simply worshipped her. He smiled and rubbed his nose. It wasn't just that she was quite pretty – there was nothing really startling about her until you looked, but then, oh my God, you saw the depths of her. Those eyes!

"Mysteries that you may never fathom, Harry my boy," he said aloud. "But oh, the chance to try!"

And what beautiful small ears she had. But never mind about that now: the problem is, what on earth is the answer to the question which that pair of lovebirds have presented to me? Or even, Eggleton, you old dimwit, what is the question?

He was at his desk, the big table littered with books and with just enough clear space for his lamp and blotter. He had begun a letter but had written no more than "My dear March" before he put down his pen and, humming through his nose, sat back to think.

Thank you, March, for sending me something I do not need or wish for, but your note was most conciliatory and perhaps ... perhaps ... my reaction to the experience at our luncheon club was somewhat extreme.

He rubbed a hand across his mouth and cheeks. But why, March, did you not bring your note to me in person? Why depute two young people to bring me a paltry peace-offering when all I needed was a word of apology?

He stood up. "No," he said aloud. "No, no. There's something more. You are keeping something from me, March. Why hold me at arm's length?"

He walked to and fro, head bowed, his hands behind his back. "No, I can't believe that. It's too..." He stopped by the fireplace. That filthy piece of rag. It can't have been an accident. March is too precise for that. So what did he mean by it? Eggleton shook his head angrily. "Pah! He cannot believe he is passing on some stupid curse, can he? Not even March can have been carried away by his researches to that extent – it's preposterous!"

He frowned. But that girl. Those eyes. She saw something and it made my blood run cold. She knew. She knew.

He lifted his head. Something outside in the garden had attracted his attention. He went to the window and peered out. The night had swallowed the lawn and made it invisible so that nothing but the ragged tops of trees showed against the stars.

He turned away.

She has read too much, that girl. He laughed quietly and shook his head. I do believe that for a moment she thought those tales of the Mary-Lou were true. That I had been chosen...

He interrupted his own thoughts by speaking aloud. "Dearie, dearie me – I am being frightened by the imaginings of a silly young girl! Eggleton, my man, act your age."

The pad of a footfall outside made him straighten, but he made himself walk to his desk. Nothing. It's nothing. Only a night sound. He put pen to paper but a sudden scurry along the side of the house had him on his feet and into the hall.

"Is that you, March!" He directed his cry to the outer door. It echoed back to him in the hall and exposed his alarm.

Something pressed against the door. There was nothing as definite as a sound but he knew that the wooden panels were holding something back.

"For God's sake, March, what trickery are you up to now!" He had regained control and his voice had steadied. He moved forward deliberately, turned the key of the door and tugged it open.

Something stepped inwards with it. Eggleton retreated, but the light of the hall was behind him and threw his shadow forward so that, for a moment, whatever it was that had entered, was obscured. But not its smell. He choked as he tried to fight it off.

Death was kind to Eggleton. The horror that

engulfed him was worse than anything he had ever dreamed, but by the time the thin, rasping fingers had reached to cover his mouth, Eggleton's heart had taken a single massive jolt and stopped.

CHAPTER
TWENTY-THREE

"There's someone to see you," said his mother.

Her expression showed it was someone she approved of, so Harry provoked her. "I'm expecting Emma. Is that who it is?"

"Emma?" The eyebrows were raised as if Mrs Hogge had never heard of her.

"Emma Judd. You know her."

His mother frowned. "Just who is she, Harry, this Emma Judd?"

He knew what the question meant. "Her father's a bus driver," he said.

"Really? How interesting." For some reason her loftiness was less scathing than he expected. "But let's not dwell on that; there's someone with your father in the office who would like to have a word with you."

It was Harry's turn to raise his eyebrows.

"It's Guy March. He seems to take an interest in you, Harry, and you know how influential he is."

Her smile was motherly. "So don't throw away *all* your chances, there's a good boy."

Guy March had a soft, friendly handshake. His smile was warm and he moved around the office of the Pheasant and Trumpet as if it was his own. It was he who asked Harry to sit down, and did so himself. Then he regarded Harry for a moment before he said, "Your father and I have just been discussing a matter of business concerning you, isn't that so, Hogge?" Harry's father, uncomfortably sidelined by what was going on and showing it, nodded. "It began as an unfortunate affair, but the outcome may be to your advantage, as I think your father will agree."

"It's a chance for you, Harry." Mr Hogge seemed about to say more but March, shifting in his seat, again took over.

"Our luncheon club has been disbanded – that sad affair on the stairs has meant that a private arrangement has become far too public." He shook his head. "We just cannot continue on the old basis, which is a great shame as your father has always made us extremely welcome here. Nevertheless, the club's work goes on." He leant forward. "And this is where you come in, young man."

"But why me?" Harry was abrupt for his father's sake. "I mean, I don't know anything about what you do."

"But you do, my boy, you do!"

A smile almost closed the pouched eyes, but

Harry was aware that he was being closely watched through the slits. Guy March must have discovered he had been eavesdropping. He reddened but said nothing.

"For one thing, Harry," March sat back and folded his hands over his stomach, "when I asked you to take my message to Mr Eggleton, you knew exactly where to go even though I had neglected to give you his name, not to mention his address. Now I wonder how that came about?"

His smile broadened to indicate that however Harry replied he would not be criticized. Nevertheless, the instant Harry opened his mouth, March wagged a finger. "No need to say a word, my boy. You used your initiative."

Harry had to keep Emma out of it. "His address wasn't difficult to find," he said. "Mr Eggleton is quite well known."

"Especially to a certain young lady."

Harry closed his eyes. The full extent of his broken promise to act alone had been exposed.

"Think nothing of it!" March was expansive. "Who can resist the wiles of women? Especially one as charming as the young lady I saw with you as I came out of the hotel." He was chuckling. He had seen it all.

"But she already knew Mr Eggleton." Harry's explanation was feeble, but he persisted. "She has worked with him."

"Worked with him?" March seemed seriously interested. "I wonder what she learned."

Harry offered no explanation.

"No matter." March drew in his breath. "And no need to say any more, my young friend. The fact is noted, and that suffices." He turned to Harry's father. "Perhaps you would like to tell him the nature of our proposal, Hogge."

Harry could see that his father was restive under March's imperious manner. Normally he would have taken Harry to task for having broken a promise, but this time he merely said, "Mr March would like you to do some secretarial work for him at the weekends. It should suit you, Harry."

"The money, Hogge, the money. Make it attractive to the young man!"

"Fifty pounds." Harry's father managed a smile. "That should help your finances."

It was more than Harry could refuse but he was given no chance to say so.

"And let us continue as we have begun." March shuffled forward in his seat. "As you will be coming to work with me I would like to present you with a little token in recognition of the good relations that have always prevailed between me and the Pheasant and Trumpet." He glanced at Mr Hogge. "Your father thinks this is altogether too excessive, but it is a whim of mine and he is too kind to deny me." He took a slim leather case from his pocket and handed it to Harry.

Harry's father was uncomfortable. "If you treat all your people with this kind of generosity, March, you will make them unemployable anywhere else. Think yourself lucky, Harry."

It was a watch. Harry opened the case and took it out.

"I'd like to see it on your wrist," said March.

The watch was an expensive one and Harry began to thank him, but once again his words were waved aside. March fussily reached forward to make sure the buckle was secure on Harry's wrist and then sat back and dismissed him. "And just be sure you are on time when next we meet; I am a harsher master than your father knows."

Emma was waiting in the market. The watch embarrassed him and did not impress her. "Does he think he owns you?" she said.

"He seems to be always giving people gifts," said Harry. He broke off, not wanting to go on.

"Who else?" she asked.

"Donovan Brett. He had a watch from Guy March and always wore it." He groaned suddenly and bowed his head. "Oh no, it's not that, is it? A rich old man giving presents to young men – what on earth's going on, Emma?"

"Not only young men, Harry. He gives presents to everybody. We took a wallet to Mr Eggleton, don't forget."

He was only slightly reassured. "I still don't like it," and he was unbuckling the strap when someone among the market crowds called Emma's name. A man at a tea stall was beckoning to her over the heads of the people, and she glanced quickly at Harry. She had become suddenly nervous.

"Is anything wrong?" he asked.

"No, of course not!" She was instantly defiant. "Come and meet my father."

Mr Judd had his peaked cap pushed to the back of his head and he grinned broadly at his daughter. "Hi there, gal. What's this, then? I thought you were at your studies." He nodded amiably at Harry, but said nothing to him.

"This is Harry, Dad."

"Oh-ah?" Mr Judd had a cigarette in one hand and a tea mug in the other. He shifted the cigarette to his mouth and stuck his hand out for Harry to grasp. "Harry," he said. "What Harry would that be?"

"Harry Hogge," said Emma. "We've been working together."

"And I'm Judd," said her father, "as if you didn't know. First name Andrew; Andy to most." He glanced down at his unbuttoned uniform jacket. "Buses. And you are...?" He was still grasping Harry's hand as a thought struck him. "Hogge? You ain't...?" and then the grin widened on each side of his cigarette. "Oh yes, you bloody are! Hogge of the Pheasant and Trumpet, that's you ... you're the landlord's boy. I seen you around when I been in that back bar in the yard. Well, bugger my heart, I'm glad to know you, Harry Hogge!" He released Harry's hand at last.

"Do you ever get to the Duke's Head?" said Harry.

"Jerry Foot's place? Of course I do."

"The beer's good."

There was a sparkle in Mr Judd's eye as he looked at Emma. "He knows my daughter and he knows his beer, he's got to be a good 'un. I should hang on to him if I was you, Em."

"Dad!" She was looking at the ground.

"She's more like her mother than me, Harry. Quiet but forceful. You'd better watch out." He laughed, threw the dregs of his mug on the ground and put his foot on his cigarette butt. "Break's over, Harry lad; take care of her." He began to move away, but suddenly thought of something. "Was you thinking of doing more of your studies with Mr Eggleton today, Emma?" She nodded, and he added, "Because if you are, you ain't."

She did not know what he meant.

"I was driving past his house this morning and there was a police car in the drive. So I asked around when we got to the garage and the boys told me he'd gone missing – door left open, letter started on his desk, but no note or nothing. Mystery."

In the avenue, the young cop on the gate was not much older than themselves, and he was not inclined to be helpful. "All I can tell you, Miss, is that the occupier has gone away without telling anyone, leaving the premises unsecure, and the neighbours got in a bit of a panic and sent for us."

"But I know Mr Eggleton. It's not like him."

"So they tell us, Miss."

"And he was..." Emma broke off because the

policeman believed he knew what she was about to say.

"You're going to tell me he was a friend of Mr Pascoe, the gentleman who was murdered a little while back." There was the ghost of a thin smile on his lips. "We are well aware of that, Miss. That's why we're here."

Emma opened her mouth to say more, but again he cut her off. "It's no use asking me any more questions. Your best bet is to give it a day or two, then get in touch with Missing Persons."

Harry had kept in the background. At least none of the policemen had connected him with Donovan Brett or the inquest, but suddenly the young cop was speaking to him. "What's up with you, mate? Seen something nasty?"

Harry had no idea it showed on his face, but he had just seen what appeared to be a thick spider web caught in the hedge beside the gate and had moved closer. He was about to point to it, but suddenly drew back because of the smell.

The cop was amused. "It don't half stink, don't it, mate? There's more of that indoors." He laughed. "Wouldn't be surprised if that's what drove the old guy out."

But Emma's attention was on Harry. Ever since they had arrived at the gate he had been scratching his wrist as if the watch was making him itch, but now, unconsciously, he was rubbing at it as if it burned.

CHAPTER
TWENTY-FOUR

The mark on his wrist remained. The watch
had been difficult to take off, clinging to him
like a manacle, and when the buckle eventually
yielded he saw that the watch-case had branded
him.

Emma looked at the red patch on his skin. "You
know what's happened," she said.

"I've been baited." He meant it as a joke, but
even as he said it his doubts returned. "Aren't we
letting it all run away with us, Emma? It's a bit
hard to believe."

"No!" She was vehement. "You've got to hand
it back to him. It's the only way."

"He'd be offended – and if he guessed the reason
he would just laugh at me."

"Harry, what have I got to do to make you see
sense? Look at everything that's happened – it's all
connected to that lunch club. Even the murder that
my aunt was sure was going to happen."

"You mean Mr Pascoe," he said. "Her voices in the head."

"I know ... I know it seems mad, but it *did* happen. And Mr Pascoe was the club's Doorman. We heard it. And now there's Mr Eggleton, he was the next Doorman, and he's vanished."

"He's not dead."

"How do we know? He was frightened when that scrap of grey stuff fell out of the letter." She bit her lip, unsure whether she should say what was in her mind. "And there's someone else." She paused, and then came out with it. "Donovan Brett. He knew something about the club because he bragged about it. And he was killed."

"He slipped and fell on a spike."

"He was given a watch," she said. "Like yours."

"How can that do any harm?" He held it up. "It's just a watch."

"Is it?"

"Of course it is – look, just a watch ... nothing more."

They bent over it. The second hand ticked around its elegant face. He turned it over, feeling foolish and on the verge of losing patience with her and her wild beliefs. The back was blank. Nothing. They were close to each other and the sensation that his mind could speak to hers returned. There's nothing to it, Emma ... see sense. But then, with a sudden flash of energy that jolted his brain and wiped out his words, she reached out and dug her nails into his palm.

"Open it!"

He tried to get his thumbnail under the back plate but it fitted too closely. They needed a knife, but he did not have one.

"Come with me," she said.

In Aunt Rose's little living room he used a table knife on the back of the watch.

"You'll bust it," said Aunt Rose.

It was more difficult than Harry thought.

"And anyway I got another job for you, young feller." She pointed to where the ironing board was still propped against the wall. "I ain't put anything back in that cupboard because it do need a new piece of lino. The smell that come through from that old cistern this morning was something terrible."

The knife found its way into the hairline crack, and Harry levered the watch open.

"It was a real horrible smell," Aunt Rose repeated, and sniffed the air. "In fact, I fancy that's come back."

Harry and Emma were both bent over the table. A waft of corruption reached them but they held their breath and did not draw back. The stench arose from a web of gauzy grey within the watch, clinging to the inside of the back plate.

"You'll have to get that lino for me, young man, or else this house won't be fit to live in."

Neither of them answered, and Harry clicked the watch closed.

"Have the cat run off with your tongues, the

pair of you?"

"Auntie," said Emma quietly, "how did you say the Mary-Lou went after its victims?"

"You know very well – they was baited."

"But how?"

"By being given something that the Mary-Lou could follow. And I'll tell you something else – once you was marked you could only get unmarked if some other person took it off you willingly."

"How would they manage to do that, Auntie?"

"That was the problem, child. They would always turn it down if they knew what it was, so you had to give it to 'em wrapped up in something."

They did not even have to look at each other. They knew what to do. "Maybe we'd better go," said Harry.

"Well, don't you go forgetting my lino, young man."

Outside, Emma reached for the watch. "No!" He drew back so sharply she was startled. "It's meant for me."

Her eyes searched his face. "I am not leaving you until we give it back to him."

Harry shrugged. "If we can get it to him we won't have to worry about it any more." Yet within himself he still debated whether it was all nonsense. He needed proof.

At a phone box he rang Barbican House. A woman answered and he asked to speak to Mr March.

"Who wants him?"

He gave his name.

"Then if you are truly Harry Hogge you are employed by him and should know where he is."

She was saying goodbye when Emma, who had her head close to Harry's, suddenly said into the mouthpiece, "Can I have a word with you, Mrs March?"

She took the phone from Harry.

"And who are you?" asked the woman.

Emma told her.

"I have heard tell of you, Emma Judd." The voice was smooth. "I don't think I wish to speak to you."

"Please, Mrs March. It's important."

"And you have been misinformed. I am not Mrs March."

"Then may I speak to her?"

"There is no Mrs March."

There was a baffling silence before the voice, seemingly pleased with the effect the denial had caused, resumed.

"I am Guy March's sister ... and we are not married!" The voice had gradually grown louder in amusement and ended in a peal of laughter. "Brother and sister! And you thought we were married!"

"But we must see you ... we must."

"Quite, quite impossible." The voice dropped and became silky, almost seductive. "We may not be married, Miss Judd, but my dear brother protects me, body and soul, as if he were my true husband."

Emma remained silent.

"If you are still there, Miss Judd, listen carefully. You waste your words to plead with me. My dear, dear brother has seen to it that I am protected from you and people such as yourself by every device known to man. Even the walls around our property are fitted with alarms, Miss Judd, and ... Miss Judd, are you still there?"

"Yes." Emma's voice was barely audible.

"You may tell your companion that the police keep an eye on Barbican House, so it is impossible for you to make any attempt to force your attention on us."

The phone clicked and was dead, but Harry was already tugging Emma from the box. His doubts had vanished. They had to act. "She was right." He was walking quickly, holding her arm. "She said I would know where he was, and I do."

They paused for breath in the foyer of the Pheasant and Trumpet. "Sometimes," Harry was anxious, "sometimes he eats here." He pushed open the door of the restaurant and peeped through. "And there he is!"

March sat alone at a corner table. Harry turned away. Anna was busy but there was a stack of hotel envelopes on the reception desk. He took one, put the watch inside and sealed it.

"Be careful, Harry! Don't antagonize him." Emma held his arm and slowed his pace as they wended their way between the tables towards March. "Smile," she murmured.

If Guy March was surprised to see them he disguised it. "Please," he said, indicating empty chairs, "do sit down."

Emma, afraid that Harry would be unable to hide his feelings, spoke first. "We are sorry to interrupt your meal, Mr March."

"Not at all, my dear. I have almost finished."

"Harry has just told me that he's going to work for you as a secretary, and we had an idea ... at least I had an idea that may be helpful."

March ate a last mouthful. "An excellent chef you have at the Pheasant and Trumpet, Harry."

Harry nodded. "What sort of work will I be doing, Mr March? Will it be connected to the history of the town?" His voice began to tail away. It was all beginning to sound artificial. "It's just that I know you are interested in that sort of thing."

"And so am I," Emma broke in. "That's why I wanted to speak to you, to see if I could help. I've already done some research." She, like Harry, was aware that her enthusiasm sounded as lame as it was. It was no more than an excuse to be near him, to get him talking.

March sat back. There was the hint of a smile on his lips, but he said nothing. Long seconds went by as he regarded them, and then he gave his response. "Very well," he said, "I shall think it over." They had failed. The interview was over. March reached for the menu.

Harry pushed back his chair and stood up. "Oh, by the way," he said, deliberately casual, "my father asked me to give you this." He held out the envelope containing the watch.

March looked up from the menu. "What is it, dear boy?"

Harry shrugged. "I don't know," and he reached further so that the envelope overlapped the menu.

"I can see it, dear boy." There was amused annoyance on March's plump face. "Put it on the table, would you?"

"He asked me to be certain I gave it to you, Mr March."

Emma watched. There was a battle of wills between them. Harry gently waved the envelope urging March to take it, but the more he thrust it forward, the more March drew back. Harry was not going to succeed.

"Mr March," she said suddenly, "Harry thinks you have been too generous to him." She put out a hand for the envelope but Harry took it out of her reach. "We have just been to see his father," she lied, "and he agrees with Harry that you should take back the watch."

Harry tore open the envelope and showed it to him. "That's all it is," he said. "I feel embarrassed about it because I haven't earned it, so would you please take it back?"

March smiled.

"I don't want it." Harry put it on the cloth and

slid it towards him.

"But it is not mine any longer – it's yours."

"Take it!" Harry pushed it suddenly towards March's fingers, but March was too quick for him. He lifted his hand out of the way, then picked up a fork from the cutlery on the table and delicately began to push the watch back towards Harry.

"You seem to be afraid to take it," said Harry.

"And why would that be, Harry?"

Emma was not quick enough to stop Harry raising his voice. "Because of the Mary-Lou!" he said.

Heads turned their way and Harry's father was coming towards them. He frowned at his son. "Harry?"

Guy March answered for him. "There's nothing for you to worry about here, Hogge. Your son and the young lady were just asking my opinion of an old folk tale, and we got rather too enthusiastic." He chuckled. "They must have heard of my interest in ancient fen monsters – in spite of my efforts to keep the *Mary-Lou* in the background." He put satirical emphasis on the name.

Harry's father was not entirely convinced. "Well, I hope he hasn't disturbed your lunch, Guy."

"Don't blame the boy, Hogge. He and the young lady must have heard some tale about the Mary-Lou – absurd name for a monster, don't you think, Harry? – and he has been wondering if the legend has become active again. However, I've put his mind at rest." He looked from Harry to Emma.

212

"Both minds at rest, I trust. Because…" He broke off as if wondering whether to continue, but then gave a self-satisfied chuckle and went on. "The legend, I fear, is a thing of the past, for the Mary-Lou could only ever come to life again if it was fed on dead men's flesh – and, I ask you, where would one get that today?"

He pushed back his chair, got up, and left. The watch remained. Harry picked it up.

CHAPTER
TWENTY-FIVE

She barely touched his lips when they kissed.
Harry's vanity said that she was inexperienced,
and she may have been; he was never sure. But
soon the feathery touch of her lips told him secrets
he had never dared to guess, enticing him into so
many mysteries that he cared about nothing else.
Neither did she. It was impossible for either of
them to take Guy March seriously.

"He's playing some sort of game with us," said
Harry. "His little secret society has collapsed so
he's looking around for someone else to frighten."

It was long after dark and they had walked aim-
lessly as they talked. Once more they came to the
Crescent and circled the high walls of Barbican
House. They looked again at the elaborate lock on
the tall gates and, in the light of the street lamps,
they could still pick out the sensors on top of the
wall.

"His sister was right about one thing," said

Emma, "it's a fortress." At the far end of the drive the house was in darkness except for one faint light in an upper window. "They are safe in there," she said, "they don't care what misery they spread with their hideous minds."

"And we took it all in," said Harry. "How could we be so stupid?" But he knew well enough. It had begun with the drip of Donovan Brett's blood onto his car, and then one tiny incident after another had built up in their minds until the appearance of the fake Mary-Lou had convinced them it had come from somewhere underground. The truth was that, whoever March had hired to act the part, had simply hidden in the hayloft waiting to be called.

"There's no passage that goes anywhere near the Pheasant and Trumpet," he said. They had searched the cellar and the hayloft itself but there was no opening to any tunnel. "It's only because someone thought it was clever to call the dining room the Sally Chamber that we began thinking of a sallyport. And all those bumps in the night were just Hobby Hobson finding something to complain about – he's got nothing else to do all night long."

And, for her part, Emma doubted Aunt Rose's voices. "She dreams away a lot of her time," she said, "and I must have got caught up in her imagination."

"So we've got nothing to worry about." Harry took the watch from his pocket. "An hour or so ago we were afraid of this," he said. "I should chuck it in the river."

"Keep it," said Emma.

"It is a sort of souvenir, I suppose."

"It's the oddest thing we've got. It may not mean what he thinks, but it means *something*."

It was too dark for him to examine the watch, but his thumb rubbed its smooth shell. "I'll even keep that stinking bit of rag inside it," he said. "If I don't have it to show to people they'll never believe that Guy March thought he could cast a spell with it." He breathed the night air. "And just because he thought I knew too much!"

"I know just as much as you."

"Then you'll be next."

They laughed, but it was still not a comfortable thought.

"He wouldn't take it back," said Harry, "no matter how much we tried." The heat of his hand had warmed the watch, and he suddenly disliked it so much that he tried to crush the glass under his thumb. "He could see that we were worried but he simply refused to touch it ... just as if *he* really believed it." Harry shook his head. "Well, if someone does believe in something as strongly as that, it does begin to get through to you."

"We are not to blame." Emma listened to the silence of the night. There was one last thing to say before Guy March drifted into the past.

"There's something that won't go out of my mind," she said. "Because it's so ugly. It was when he was talking about the Mary-Lou. He said it would only come to life if it was fed on human flesh ... and then he made a sort of joke about it and said where could you be expected to get human flesh these days? It was the smug smile he had on his face, Harry, as though he really did know where he could get it." She shuddered. "Dead bodies, Harry – it's awful!"

Dead bodies. Coffins. Undertakers. The spark ran from word to word and Harry suddenly stopped short. Coffins. The Duke's Head. The undertaker's man in the corridor.

"The coffin." He faced Emma. "When Guy March's secretary died the coffin stayed all night at Barbican House ... in the castle ruins. I heard the man say so. And next day, when the undertakers came to take it away, they lifted it up and it was too light ... far too light!"

The Crescent's great arms curved around them. The whole night was focused where they stood, and all their scattered fears began to piece together once more, galloping in upon them, jostling until they fitted together, detail by detail until no reasoning could destroy what faced them. The Mary-Lou had been fed. And unless they got the watch into Guy March's hands within the next few hours they were condemned.

Harry made one last attempt to drag them back from the edge. "Even if it's true," he tried to hide the thought of some monstrously perverted creature feeding on corpses, "even if it's all true, and is happening just there," he pointed to the wall of the big house, "the only thing March has got to do if he wants to set his creature on to someone else is to open the gates and let it out. There's no need for a secret way."

"No, that's wrong, Harry." Emma's mind was racing, afraid of what she was saying but even more afraid of keeping it to herself. "He would risk too much by just letting it loose. He doesn't want anybody to know too much, especially not now. He doesn't even have his dining club in your hotel any more. If they ever were helpful to him they aren't of any use to him now – he's murdered two of them, Harry ... as well as Donovan."

She was convinced of it, and she shook his arm, forcing him to see what she saw. "He's connected with all of them ... *all* of them, and people will soon see it and start asking questions. He has got to be able to do it secretly. There's got to be a way out of the grounds of his house that nobody knows."

If there was a way out, there was a way in.

Harry tilted his head as if he studied the sky. Could she be right? Should they go to the police? Was the story too wild? Did they have time?

There was a moon, and clouds lay like amber coastlines above the rooftops. Amber except where they crossed the face of the moon and lay like grey plumes. Wisps of grey. Grey gauze. His nostrils seemed to pick up the reek of the grey fragments inside his watch; and the stench that arose from the cistern in the cupboard.

He lowered his eyes. Her face was a pearly smoothness in the darkness. "I know where we have to go," he said.

CHAPTER
TWENTY-SIX

They were the only walkers in Moat Lane, and when they came to the little square it was utterly silent. Aunt Rose's house was dark and asleep.

"She goes to bed early," said Emma.

"We'll just have to wake her."

"No." She took a key from the pocket of her skirt. "She makes me carry this so I can get in to see her at any time."

The key rattled in the lock but the door swung silently open, and he followed her into the blackness of the passage where he had to feel his way past the hazards that had made him stumble the first time.

"Wait," she whispered and she crept into the living room ahead of him and switched on the light. The grey cat did not so much as blink. It watched them from Aunt Rose's chair but did not move as Harry went forward to the cupboard and opened it. His shadow fell over the cistern, but he silently thanked Aunt Rose for leaving her torch handy. She knew it would be needed when he fitted the new lino for her.

The cistern cover lifted easily, and the reek of corruption was less than before. New doubts crowded his mind. The stone projections from the side of the shaft now seemed much more like rough workmanship than the steps he had imagined they were, and a curious fold in the stonework that he thought could have been a gap seemed no more than a shadow thrown by the torch. If there had been a gap, how could Aunt Rose's father have missed it?

"There's got to be something," Emma insisted, but she wanted to hold him back when he took off his jacket and sat on the edge of the opening.

"I'll have to go down and see what there is to see." He put the watch in his trouser pocket, and the strap of the torch around his wrist as though there was no turning back once he started. Then he lowered himself into the shaft, feeling for the protrusions with his feet. They were hardly steps, but the shaft was narrow and he could straddle it and work his way down, little by little.

His hands were still clinging to the rim when he paused. She heard him grunt as though something puzzled him.

"What is it?"

"My feet seem to be on a ledge."

She saw him bend forward, directing the torch towards his feet. Then, quite suddenly, he moved sideways and seemed to melt into the wall.

"Harry!" She lay on her face, looking down. "What's happening?"

"I found it!" His voice came from the empty shaft. Then his head appeared, seeming to come through the solid stonework. "There's a passage cut sideways so you can't make it out from up there. I'll see where it goes."

"Wait!" She was not as tall as Harry and her feet had difficulty finding the ledge, but he got his arm around her and guided her into the gap.

Air blew into their faces. It had the taint of ancient places but the foulness, like an old trail, had diminished. The torch beam showed a narrow passage with an arched roof dwindling into the distance, and Emma was sure where it led; it fitted everything she knew. "It goes under the Crescent," she whispered. "It must come out inside the castle."

Harry was thinking ahead. Even if she was right, he still had to get to Guy March. He knew he should tackle that problem alone, face to face with March, but the jerk of her head when he suggested it made it seem like an insult. They were going to need each other, and Emma knew it.

They walked in single file with the darkness closing in behind Emma's back. The dust they trod in could have come from the work of the masons who made the tunnel, but the floor was smooth enough and they did not stumble. Harry's shoulders prevented her seeing ahead and she tried, by counting footsteps, to calculate when they had crossed the little square outside her aunt's house, and when they were moving beneath the gardens and houses of the Crescent, and then when it was the road itself above them. It took longer than she thought, and she had reckoned they had just crossed the road and were beneath the wall when Harry stopped. He, too, thought they had entered the grounds of Barbican House.

The thought that they were deep underground seemed suddenly to make the walls press in to squeeze the breath from Emma's lungs, and her heart pounded. Harry heard her gasp and he turned and put his arm through hers. "I can see the end," he murmured and they went forward like a single creature, clinging to each other.

The tunnel seemed to resist their progress, and it was some moments before they realized that they were walking uphill, coming up towards the castle mound. And the tunnel ended in a wall. It was of solid stone, but at its foot there was a square, dark hole. They crouched beside it, listening, and when no sound reached them he advanced his torch into the gap.

There was space beyond the wall and they saw the large block of stone that had been removed to make the hole. Harry put his shoulders through the gap. "There's a bigger tunnel," he said, "going away to the right." To the left it was blocked by a fall of stone.

It was Emma who recognized where they were.

"It's the passage that goes into the grounds," she whispered. It was years since the school visit, but she was able to visualize the passage into the garden. "We can get to the house from there."

The block of stone that lay on the floor on the other side had been pulled away far enough for Harry and then Emma to squeeze through. The block was cold to the touch and when she stood beside it and saw how long it was her mind registered the fact that it was far longer than was necessary to simply plug the gap. And it stank.

On the far side of the lawn, a door opened at the back of the house.

"There is a moon tonight, my love, and the heavens are gorgeous."

"Is there dew on the grass, dearest one?" In her room she cut the deck and dealt the cards. "It is long years since I saw dew."

"Your feet would print it prettily, my dear, but you are too precious to risk the cruel air."

"You are my eyes and ears."

"And I shall scatter dewdrops for you." March crossed the lawn and looked back at the prints he had made in the grass. "We have walked through the night together," he said. "I am at the gate."

Emma took the torch from Harry and directed it on to the block of stone. She saw what it was and shuddered. "It's a coffin," she muttered. "They used a stone coffin to seal the wall." She stooped to look at the lid. Marks of damage showed along its edge, and iron hooks and a pulley had been rigged to raise or lower it. And at some time it had been opened; the smell told them that. The lid was closed, but they knew what the coffin contained.

Harry spoke through clenched teeth to prevent himself shivering. "We haven't much time!" He had to act fiercely or turn tail and run. He grabbed roughly at her arm and dragged her away from the coffin. "We can't hang about. We've got to find him and take him by surprise – force him to take the watch!" Neither of them knew how it was to be done.

The air current still blew in their faces and they turned their backs on the coffin and headed away from it, stumbling sometimes in their haste to get into the open.

There was a side tunnel. Harry missed it, but Emma saw it and was confused. It was perhaps a turning they should take. She snatched at the torch and directed it into the opening. It was a blind passage, no more than a deep alcove, but it was occupied.

And there was a face.

The beam fell full on it. She smothered a cry and started back, but the face was peaceful, as if it slept. She recognized it. Her old teacher stood in the centre of the alcove, with his eyes closed. And then he moved. He swayed slightly, the torch dipped and its light fell on what was left of James Eggleton below the neck.

Emma clamped a hand over her mouth and whimpered, screaming a thin scream into her palm, as the rags of torn flesh and streaked bone revolved slowly. The half-eaten corpse was skewered on a butcher's hook.

In her room, the woman at the card table shuffled and dealt. "The cards are sluggish tonight," she murmured.

At the gate March turned slowly, probing the deep shadows of the dark garden. "The night is silent, my love, and nothing stirs."

"The cards will not be kind." Her voice had become peevish. "That boy is the Knave of Clubs but he lurks in my hand and will not show his face! He is a deceitful, cunning, creeping, vile slitherer in the night and he must be dealt with!"

"There is nothing for you to fear, little one." March licked his dry lips and his eyes darted anxiously at the banks of shadow. "I have a sure remedy for any lurking boy who may disturb your dreams … something which will track him down before this night is out, no matter where he is."

"He hides from me." She was hardly aware of what he said. "That boy is hidden! You must take care!"

Deep within the tunnel they heard the rattle of the key and the clash of iron as the gate swung open. And then a flashlight in the distance glared, swung and stabbed again.

If they retreated they would be seen. There was only one place to go. The breath shuddered in their throats as they approached the hanging corpse. Cold, damp fragments clung to them as they squeezed their way past and stood behind it, wide-eyed and motionless. James Eggleton was their only protection.

Laughter came ahead of the approaching foot-steps, and then a voice that seemed to quarrel with its own echo. "I have a dainty friend that will seek him out, don't fear." But the voice and the laughter were forced. March was reluctant to be where he was but tried to make light of it. "This is rather a dreadful place, my love." But he fell silent as he approached the alcove, knowing what was there.

Harry felt Emma shrink against his side. He put his arm around her, but it was not fear alone that swept over her. She had heard more than March's words. There was another voice, higher-pitched and speaking with so insistent a whisper that it pierced her head. "The cards are speaking at last!" it said. "The King is in his kingdom."

"So he is, my love."

"And now I play a Knave! The boy has arrived. He is close."

"And baited!" March raised his voice, giving himself courage. "He tried to pass it on to me – and I am the one person who is immune. The bait remains with him. I cannot be touched!"

"But take care, my dearest. He is close. His card is next to yours."

The torch beam flickered at the mouth of the alcove. "Next to me," said March, "is my sad old friend." The torch picked out the torn flesh and its beam wavered. "What a dreadful sight my old friend is. He is frightful to look on!" Panic caught at his voice. "This is an awful place!"

"Coward!" The word jarred in Emma's head, and in the room the woman threw the cards across the table. "No kingdom is got without blood! Let loose the beast and send the boy to hell!"

The beam descended from the corpse and raked across the floor. It touched their feet. They held still.

"A charnel house." March spoke to himself. "My kingdom is a charnel house and will not let me go."

The woman's voice, coaxing now, murmured in Emma's ear. "Take heart. If the world is a charnel house you are its master. Nothing can touch you … release your servant and eliminate the boy."

The torch beam swept away, and March, still muttering, went deeper into the tunnel.

Once more they edged past the body and saw March silhouetted against the patch of light as he approached the stone coffin. Harry was beginning to move after him when Emma caught his arm and tugged him back.

"No!" Her whisper was a command. "We can't do anything here. We've got to get to the house!" She dug her nails into his arm and he had to go with her.

They had to feel their way along the wall but soon a faint grey patch ahead showed them the gate. It was unlocked. They eased it open and gently closed it behind them, and then found themselves shuddering so violently that for a while they could not walk.

"His sister." Emma gulped the night air, clearing her lungs. "Give the watch to her."

Harry's mind spun, not understanding.

"March can't be baited," she gasped, "but his sister can!"

They crossed the lawn and Emma was looking up at the single window where a light shone when she heard the female voice again. "Stay silent, my dear," it said. "We must listen." And then silence.

Emma leant towards Harry. "They know we aren't far away," she whispered.

"How do they know?"

"They talk." She put a finger over his lips to stop him asking questions. "We haven't much time."

They looked back towards the castle mound. It was hunched and innocent, but deep within it a corpse hung, and a coffin lid was being raised.

They found the door that March had left ajar. They went through and closed it behind them. Now they could use the torch. They crossed a stone-flagged kitchen and found their way into the hall.

A broad staircase ascended into the yawning heart of the house, but no sound came from above. Harry switched off the torch. Windows gave enough grey light and they began to climb. Carpet deadened their footsteps, and the heavy banister rail guided them.

From outside they had seen that her room was two floors up. At the first landing the staircase turned and they went up into parts of the house where strangers did not penetrate. They listened again, and heard nothing. But now a new dilemma faced them. How, when they confronted her, were they going to act? They put their heads close, intending to whisper, but the whole stairwell seemed to be listening, so Harry guided Emma to a doorway and turned the handle. There was a faint click, and the door swung back to let them through. He shielded the beam to a pencil and looked around. A dressing table, a tall, dark wardrobe, chairs and a bed. A mattress without bedclothes. The room was unused and they could whisper together.

"I'll force the watch into her hands," he said. He could think of nothing else.

Emma shook her head. "That won't work. She's got to take it from you, willingly."

"But how?" He saw no way to do it.

"Give the watch to me. I stand a better chance." He refused. "Then give me the torch!" She snatched it from him and went to the dressing table and shone it on the pots and little china trays. He tried to ask what she was doing but she would not be interrupted. There was a decorated china box and her hand darted towards it and lifted the lid.

"Manicure set," she muttered. "Nail file." She handed the file to him. "Open the watch," she said. "Take out that grey stuff – that's the bait. Give that to her."

He again asked how it was to be done.

"Just do what I say! We haven't time for anything else."

She held the torch while he stabbed the file at the back of the watch. The back sprang open, and as it did so Emma reached forward and lifted out the grey gauze. "It's mine now." She turned away, folding it in her handkerchief.

They both knew what she had done. "I can't let you!" He put his hand over hers, but she clamped her fist on the bait.

"It's our only chance. I'll get it to her while you try to give her the watch."

They ran together up the final flight of stairs, careless now of what noise they made. A thread of light showed under a door. Harry gripped the handle and, when Emma nodded, he pushed the door open.

Warmth took them by surprise. And soft lights. Lamps in rosy shades gleamed on furniture spaced for elegance, and glinted on the ribbed gilding of a small table where a woman looked up suddenly from her cards. She wore a night-dress, but swiftly drew her robe around herself and sat facing them with her arms crossed over her bosom, her eyes wide, and her mouth rounded in a little pout of surprise.

Harry halted. They had blundered. The woman who sat cosily in front of the fire in her boudoir playing solitaire had a soft and gentle face, delicate and defenceless. He was on the point of backing away when Emma spoke. "Miss March?"

"Yes, dear." If she had been surprised in the first place, the woman had soon overcome it. "Who are you?"

"We have come to return something to you, Miss March." Emma and Harry crossed the carpet and stood in front of the card table.

"Oh, you do look so threatening, standing there," said Miss March. "I hope you don't intend me any harm." A smile struggled to her lips, making her look like a child attempting to pacify bullies. And it was necessary to coax her.

Harry forced himself to sound apologetic. "All we want to do," he said, "is to return this. It belongs to your brother."

"Guy?" But the question was not addressed to them. She was gazing at the ceiling. "They have arrived with a watch which they hope to give me … and I am so worried!" Harry held out the watch to her, but she sat back in her seat, unwilling to touch or be touched.

"Put it on the table," said Emma, and reached across to point to the spot. "Leave it there, and let's go." She turned away but, as she did so, her hand brushed the deck of cards and they fell to the floor. She stooped to gather them as Harry put the watch on the table top. Then, as he had done with her brother, he began to slide it towards Miss March.

"Please take it," he pleaded.

Emma, out of sight, slid the scrap of grey into the deck of cards and stood up.

"Come away." She held Harry's arm. "We've done all we can." As she turned away she held out the cards. "I'm sorry," she said.

"That's quite all right, dear." Miss March looked at the cards in Emma's hand. "Just put them on the table." And she again raised her eyes to the ceiling. "Guy," she sighed, "I think the time has come." She stood up and motioned them to wait, while she remained silent, listening.

Somewhere below in the empty house a door opened and closed.

They heard slow footsteps coming up the stairs. She smiled at them. "It's Guy," she said. "He's not as young as he used to be, poor lamb."

Whatever it was on the stairs kept up the same steady pace. Now there was a shuffling slide to the footsteps as if garments rustled. "He gets out of breath," she said, "sweet man."

They stood gazing at the open door and they heard him gasping as he reached the landing.

"Darling," she called, "are you alone – or is there someone with you?"

"I have a companion, my love."

"How wonderful!" Excitedly she looked from Emma to Harry and confided in them. "I know who it is, but I have never seen him because I have all I need in this room with my cards." Emma, with the cards still in her hand, held them out to her. Absently, Miss March took them. "My cards and my brother, they are all I ever need, do you understand, my darlings? So tonight is a treat, something I never expected to witness." She lifted her voice. "Bring in your companion, dearest, so that our guests may see him."

There was a light footstep on the landing and a figure appeared in the darkness of the doorway.

Enraptured, Miss March gasped and raised her clenched hands under her chin.

The figure crossed the threshold and the doorway became an open grave. Disintegration reeked in the maggoty profusion of the creature's lips, and its sinews, visible where its skin had flaked away, tautened and slackened on joints of naked bone as it moved its limbs and advanced.

"Welcome," said Miss March, and she called out to her brother, "Come in, Guy. We shall watch your servant earn his supper."

Her hands, still clasped beneath her chin, fidgeted with the cards like a little girl at a pantomime.

Emma, from the corner of her eyes, saw the expression on Miss March's face change. Disgust tugged at the corners of her mouth and was displaced by a moment of puzzlement as she looked down at the cards. And then, sweeping away all else, terror ruined every feature. The card uppermost in her hand bore a scrap of grey.

"No!" Her shriek seemed to dim the light. "No!"

Harry and Emma drew back and allowed the Mary-Lou to walk to its victim.

"This is not mine!" Miss March came forward, holding out the card and its scrap of grey. "It belongs to the girl! I give it back to the girl!" She tried to do so, stretching towards Emma. But her hand could not reach far enough. Her new guest was in the way, waiting to embrace her.

The yellow teeth were on her, and in her, before March, whimpering like a puppy, overflowing with fear, came scampering forward and laid his hands upon the mess of stinking rags and bones that engulfed his sister. He saw what it was doing to her and, with a roar that rent his throat, fury burst through his fear.

March clutched a shining fire iron from the hearth, raised it high and brought it down across the creature's neck. Its shoulders jerked awkwardly, the head drooped, but it kept at its gnawing work, snuffling and grunting as it bit and tore.

He struck again. The iron passed through the neck bones of the creature, and the severed head, twisting from the force of the blow, curved through the air and bedded itself in the burning coals of the grate. There was a sputtering hiss as what hair remained on the skull flared and fled, then teeth cracked and spat in the heat, and the eye sockets boiled while the mouth gushed flame so fierce it shrieked.

They could never recall their flight down the stairs. The first thing they knew was that they were gulping the night air as if nothing else could purify them, and as they climbed the gate every alarm rang out and echoed and re-echoed against the silent fronts of the Crescent. But by the time anyone arrived they were gone.

EPILOGUE

They came to the top of the lane and looked out over the valley.

"One day," said Harry, "we shall tell someone about it all."

Emma saw that rain was coming, misting the hills and spreading secrecy over the valley. "But we can't say anything yet," she said. Other people, police, newspapers had made their own decisions … it had all been the work of a madman who had ended up killing his sister in a frenzy. The truth lay elsewhere, and the path Emma and Harry had trodden to reach it was too tortuous for others to follow; too deep a secret.

They never mentioned Guy March by name. "He's gone for good," said Harry. "They'll never let him free."

When March was found in his sister's room, with charred bones and tattered chaos around him, the whirlwind in his brain had tightened and frozen. He had never spoken.

The first spots of rain touched Emma's forehead and she tilted her face to the sky. This had happened before with another girl.

"You gave her your coat," said Emma. It was in his mind and she had read his thoughts as clearly as if he had spoken. It still happened, and he did not want it to end.

"I only came here because I had to go back to the beginning," he said. It was across the valley that they had seen Donovan Brett's yellow jersey.

The rain increased and he took off his jacket, but she would not take it. The rain smoothed her black hair to her cheeks and simplified her face. She shivered. He put his arm around her and they stood together like statues in a fountain and let themselves be drenched.

GILRAY'S GHOST
John Gordon

"One of your pupils is dead and another, I think, is in danger."

"What kind of danger?"

"Great danger. A ghost doth yearn to take her life away."

In a tomb in the forest lies the body of evil necromancer Doctor Septimus Carr, whose grisly experiments claimed the life of a servant girl. Now, two centuries later, another girl is in mortal danger. Enter Gilray. This quirky time traveller has flown back to prevent the looming wickedness. But it's no simple task. For a start, who is the girl – Linda Blake, Pauline Withers, Cassandra Ashe...? Their teacher – flirtatious Bob Wheatley – is the man whose help Gilray needs most, but he's preoccupied with passionate affairs of his own. Meanwhile, the sinister Rosa and Robin Underleaf are planning to resurrect their "Master"...

Thrilling, intricate, highly entertaining, this tale of horror and desire builds to an intense and chilling climax.

THIRSTY
Matthew T. Anderson

"When you get thirsty, you get angry without reason. Increasingly. You feel prone to violence. You feel prone to drink blood..."

Chris just wants to be a normal guy – to hang out with his friends Tom and Jerk, avoid his bickering parents, get a date with Rebecca Schwartz. Lately, though, he's had this strange, abnormal desire, a thirst for blood... Chris is turning into a vampire. He needs help – but who can he trust? Chet, the oddly cynical Celestial Being? His friends? His family? Can he even trust himself? Time is running out and Chris is so thirsty...

Suspenseful, darkly humorous, Matthew T. Anderson's sharp-toothed tale of terror and teen angst will keep readers gripped to the last, blood-curdling page.

MAPHEAD
Lesley Howarth

Greetings from the Subtle World –

Twelve-year-old MapHead is a visitor from the Subtle World that exists side by side with our own. Basing himself in a tomato house, the young traveller has come to meet his mortal mother for the first time. But, for all his dazzling alien powers, can MapHead master the language of the human heart?

Highly Commended for the Carnegie Medal and shortlisted for the WH Smith Mind Boggling Books Award.

"Weird, moving and funny by turns... Lesley Howarth has a touch of genius."
Chris Powling, Books for Keeps

"Offbeat and original... Strongly recommended to all who enjoy a good story."
Books For Your Children

MAPHEAD 2
Lesley Howarth

If you could go anywhere – do *any*thing – where would you go? What would you do?

This is the dilemma facing MapHead on his return to Rubytown from his home in the Subtle World. Materializing in a multi-storey car park, he is drawn to the Stamp family, for whom, he feels, he has a vital task to perform. But what? And how? Using his powers to flash maps across his head is one thing; using them to intrude in people's lives is something else. That can only cause problems – big problems... Soon Map-Head finds himself up the multi without a ticket – and, this time, without his dad to help him!

"A story full of charm and humour."
The Daily Mail

LONE WOLF
Kristine L. Franklin

Three years ago, following a family tragedy, Perry Dubois and his dad left the city and moved to a remote cabin in the American woods. Here in wolf country, they lead a solitary life. Perry doesn't even go to school, spending much of his time with his dog, Rhonda, in the cave that's his secret hideout. Then Willow Pestalozzi and her large family move into the empty house nearby and Perry finds his world invaded. For Willow is full of questions – questions that remind Perry of everything he's tried so hard to forget. She wants to be friends, but Perry doesn't need anyone, does he? He's a loner like the wolf he hears howling in the woods. And yet there's something about the Pestalozzis, with their mess and noise and warmth, that draws him in...

Kristine L. Franklin's absorbing and touching story reveals how learning to laugh again also means being able, at last, to cry.

GROOSHAM GRANGE
Anthony Horowitz

"There's something nasty going on at Groosham Grange…"

David Eliot's new school is a very weird place indeed. New pupils are made to sign their names in blood; the French teacher disappears every full moon; the assistant headmaster keeps something very chilling in his room… There are many strange questions to be answered. Most important of all, how on earth can David get away – *alive*?

"One of the funniest books of the year."
Young Telegraph

"Hilarious … speeds along at full tilt from page to page." *Books for Keeps*

THE SWITCH
Anthony Horowitz

"Tad opened his mouth to cry out. The boy did the same. And that was when he knew… He wasn't looking at a window. He was looking at a *mirror*."

Tad Spencer, only son of a fabulously rich businessman, has everything a boy could wish for. But one evening he makes the major mistake of wishing he was someone else. A switch takes place and when he wakes, he's Bob Snarby, trapped in a cruel and squalid funfair world inhabited by petty criminals, mysterious fortune-tellers and the murderous Finn. Worse is to follow, though, as Tad is subjected to monstrous experiments, uncovering home truths that put his very life in danger…

"A formidably well-written adventure story, every bit as exciting as anything by Dahl or Blyton."
The Independent

THE BEAST OF WHIXALL MOSS
Pauline Fisk

At the age of eleven, Jack is resigned to his world.

So what if he can never satisfy his mother's desire for perfection and his brother can? So what if he's lonely out on Whixall Moss? He doesn't care – or so he likes to tell himself. Then one day he sees, in a boat hidden on the creek, a beautiful, fabulous beast. At once he is filled with a wild longing: he must own it. But the boat's mysterious inhabitants have other ideas...

Gripping and powerful, this novel by Smarties Book Prize Winner Pauline Fisk is a tale that will live long in the imagination.

FIRE, BED AND BONE
Henrietta Branford

The year is 1381 and unrest is spreading like plague.

England's peasants are tired of the hardship and injustice they suffer at the hands of harsh landlords. Rebellion is in the air, bringing dramatic and violent upheaval to the lives of families like Rufus, Comfort and their children – and even to dogs, like the old hunting bitch who is the narrator of this unforgettable tale.

This gripping and vivid story by a Smarties Book Prize-winning author is an extraordinary achievement, depicting the tumult and tragedy of the Peasants' Revolt through the eyes, ears and nose of a dog.